one time

ALSO BY SHARON CREECH

Walk Two Moons

Absolutely Normal Chaos

Pleasing the Ghost

Chasing Redbird

Bloomability

The Wanderer

Fishing in the Air

Love That Dog

A Fine, Fine School

Ruby Holler

Granny Torrelli Makes Soup

Heartbeat

Who's That Baby?

Replay

The Castle Corona

Hate That Cat

The Unfinished Angel

The Great Unexpected

The Boy on the Porch

Moo

Saving Winslow

SHARON CREECH

one time

JOANNA COTLER BOOKS
An Imprint of HarperCollinsPublishers

Library of Congress Cataloging-in-Publication Data

Names: Creech, Sharon, author.
Title: One time / Sharon Creech.
Description: First edition. | New York, NY : HarperCollins, [2020] |
    Audience: Ages 8-12. | Audience: Grades 4-6. | Summary: Imaginative,
    eleven-year-old Gina, her mysterious new neighbor, Antonio, and their
    classmates are inspired by an unusual young teacher to see who they
    are and envision who they are meant to become.
Identifiers: LCCN 2019043995 | ISBN 9780062570741 (hardcover) |
    ISBN 9780062570758 (library binding) | ISBN 9780062570765 (pbk.)
Subjects: CYAC: Imagination—Fiction. | Teachers—Fiction. | Schools—
    Fiction. | Family life—Fiction.
Classification: LCC PZ7.C8615 One 2020 | DDC [Fic]—dc23
LC record available at https://lccn.loc.gov/2019043995

Typography by Laura Mock
21 22 23 24 25 BRR 10 9 8 7 6 5 4 3 2 1
❖
First paperback edition, 2021

To all the Stretchberrys and Lightstones
who light the way

*Tell me, what is it you plan to do
with your one wild and precious life?*

—MARY OLIVER

CONTENTS

one time

TELL ME

~⁀❧

I wonder about you: who are you?

Dear Miss Lightstone:

I am Gina Filomena, age eleven.

    Sometimes teachers think I am not paying attention, but what they mean is that I am not paying attention to *them*. I pay attention to lots of other things like what is happening outside the windows, and the noises in the room, like the humming and the tapping and the snapping and the sniffling, and all the smells—some good, some bad. But I will try to pay attention to *you.*

I will try.

Your student,
Gina F.

When the new teacher asked us to write something about ourselves, that's what I wrote. I did not write about the angels or the boy with the visions.

No need to scare her.

NEW NEIGHBORS

A month before school began, new neighbors and their cat moved into the house next door. When I spotted the cat sitting forlornly on Dad's parsley plants, I tried to pet it, but the fur on its back shot straight up. A tall boy appeared from behind the moving truck and snatched the cat.

"That's Mr. Blue. You don't want to touch him," he said. "Cat is mean as spit."

The boy seemed about my age. Hard to tell.

He was tall and lean but not skinny, and he moved as if his bones and joints were loosely connected. His hair was black and curly, shorter on the sides and longer on top so that it flopped over his forehead on one side. His eyes were black and shiny, his skin so smooth. In one hand, he held a jackknife and in the other hand a small piece of wood.

I liked that boy from the minute I saw him. There was something calm and relaxed about him, something kind, but most appealing was his smile: a wide, gleaming, welcoming smile.

Later, when I thought about that smile and its effect on me, I realized that people didn't often smile in that open, inviting way. When I met Antonio with that generous smile, I was caught off guard, stunned. Maybe you would have been, too.

"You going to live there?" I asked.

"Guess so." He nodded at my house. "You

going to live over *there*?"

"I already do. I'm Gina."

He tapped his chest. "Antonio."

An older girl came out onto the porch, scowling. "Nut head! We need some help here!" Later I learned that she was Carlotta, his cousin, and that his grandmother also was moving in.

I didn't see much of the new neighbors the first week they were there. Occasionally I heard someone calling for Mr. Blue, but by the time I made it to the window, the cat was already dashing into their opened door.

I asked my dad what he thought about the new neighbors.

He rubbed his hands together and leaned toward me. "Ah! Spies, you think?"

My father liked to speculate.

One time, at the grocery, when a clerk took a long time ringing up our order, Dad wondered if she was tapping in an extra code. He examined the receipt closely as we left the store. "Maybe there's a coded message here, like 'Help me. I've been kidnapped.'"

Oddly, that's kind of how I felt when I saw that Antonio boy, that maybe he was sending out coded messages into the air, through that smile. I felt a strong pull to help that boy, whether he actually needed my help or not.

THE ANGEL, THE GROUBES, AND THE CLACKERTYS

~o

My grandmother, Nonna Filomena, liked to tell stories about the feisty and moody Angel Lucia who lived "high up in the mountains of Italy, where the earth is the color of chocolate and the sky the purest blue."

One time, when the townspeople in the village below were bickering over a piece of land, Angel Lucia threw down buckets of hail—right in the middle of summer.

Another time, Angel Lucia pecked holes in all

the pies sitting on windowsills to cool because one cook had denied a beggar a piece of fresh pie.

One time Angel Lucia swept through the town, snipping flowers from yards and gathering them into a bouquet for a poor girl who was getting married but had no money for a bouquet.

I never doubted the angel, no matter how outrageous the tales about her were. I welcomed her, adored her, depended on her.

Not everyone appreciated Angel Lucia. My mother, for instance, might say, "Really? *Really?* Maybe Angel Lucia was hungry for pie." Or, "*Really?* I'd like Angel Lucia to throw down some hail on the Groubes."

The Groubes were the family who used to live next door, before the new neighbors moved in. They had three angry, nasty boys who swore and threw eggs on houses and whacked people with sticks and left stinky garbage rotting in their driveway. Dad told me to ignore them and said that if Angel Lucia could hear them, she would coat their tongues with molasses so they would stick to the roofs of their mouths.

I was relieved when the Groubes moved out and the new neighbors with that tall Antonio boy moved in. They made no noise whatsoever.

This did not mean the whole neighborhood was now quiet because at the other end of Hatch Street lived the Clafferty family with seven or eight children (hard to count) and a little yippy-yappy dog. Dad called them the "Clackertys." The kids ran around shouting and fighting, and the parents yelled at them to be quiet or get inside or go outside or quit hitting/punching/spitting/throwing, and the little dog yipped and yapped and yipped and yapped. I walked or ran the long way around the block rather than pass by their house.

THE LIGHT, THE POLLEN,
AND THE ELEPHANT

~

A few days after the neighbors moved in, I was mowing the grass when Antonio came outside. He walked to the back of his yard, peered into the bushes, and crept along the tree line.

"You looking for Mr. Blue?" I asked.

"Nope. Did you see anything strange out here this morning, like anything growing fast or dripping pollen?"

"Um, no."

He was wearing a white T-shirt and black

shorts. That skin—it was so smooth. He smiled that smile.

He said, "Last night, I saw a white light, bigger than the moon, lighting up the black sky. It was surrounded by an orange halo, and it sped above the trees"—he waved his arm across the sky—"and it changed shape from round to thin and flat, like a pancake."

"A pancake?"

"And it was so bright, so bright, and then it was gone."

"I wonder what it was."

"After it left, the tops of the trees right there were blackened." He gestured toward the trees. "And tall, thick green stems sprouted from the earth and grew taller and taller, until they were as tall as—well, as tall as me!"

"As tall as you?" I looked toward where he had motioned.

"And velvety red flowers blossomed, dripping

yellow pollen. Right there." His hands made circles in the air and his fingers wiggled down, down.

I saw nothing: no blackened trees, no sprouting plants, no red blossoms dripping. "But now?" I said. "Where—?"

"All gone! But it happened and I saw it."

Two days later, when I was taking out the trash, Antonio's cousin, Carlotta, called to me from their back door.

"You!" she said. "Have you seen Antonio?"

"Hi. I'm Gina—"

"Have you seen Antonio?"

"No. Is he—"

The door closed abruptly.

From behind the bushes, up popped Antonio. He put a finger to his mouth. "Shh."

"I guess you don't want to be found," I said.

"Right." Antonio acted as if he were resuming

a conversation. "So, yesterday I saw the elephant."

"The elephant? What elephant?"

"The one down the street."

"I've never seen an elephant on this street."

"You haven't? Well, maybe he's new. Anyway, I saw a frog sitting on his head."

I thought maybe I wasn't hearing correctly. "A frog? On the elephant's head?"

"Yes, and the elephant raised his trunk and felt around the top of his head"—here Antonio felt around the top of his own head in imitation—"until the elephant reached the frog, and then he gathered it up in his trunk and set it down on the ground. Gently. As if it were a child."

He smiled that smile. I expected little flashes of light to sparkle off his teeth.

"An elephant. A frog. I wish I'd seen that." I leaned toward him and whispered, "Do you need help of any kind?"

"No," he whispered back. "Do you?"

"No."

When I told my parents about Antonio seeing the elephant, my mother said, "Really? An *elephant*?" She glanced out the window. "Haven't seen any elephants around here today, or, well, *ever*."

Dad said, "But you never know. When did that boy see the elephant?"

"Yesterday, I think."

"Let's go for a walk," Dad said, already pulling on his jacket. "See if we can spot any elephants."

So we walked down the street, past a dozen small bungalows like ours and past the noisy Clackertys (two kids up in a tree, shouting at another on the ground below them; one kicking a trash can up the driveway; two throwing rubber balls against the house; one banging on the door and shouting, "Let me in! Let me in!"; and the little dog trailing its red leash and yipping and yapping and nipping at ankles). We walked the length of the street and around the block, all the way back to our house.

"No elephant," Dad pronounced. "I bet someone stole it."

"Dad!"

"Probably one of the Clackertys."

NONNA FILOMENA, THE ANGEL, AND THE FIGHT

Each year on my birthday, Nonna Filomena, my grandmother who lived in Italy, sent me updates on Angel Lucia and also something colorful to wear—a scarf or blouse or skirt—made of delicate materials and unusual colors mixed together: deep crimson and emerald green or cobalt blue and bright gold.

No one else in town wore this sort of clothing and for my first few years of school, the other kids took no notice of my clothes, just as I did not take much notice of theirs. It wasn't until I was eight or nine that they began to comment. Some mocked me. Others imitated me, arriving with colorful scarves or bright blouses or sweaters, but the clothing I had was not easily copied, not from stores near us.

One time, a mother made her way to our house and pleaded her case with my parents.

"It isn't fair," the mother said. "My daughter whines all day long: 'Why can't I have clothes like Gina's? Why can't I have colorful scarves?' It's driving me insane. Please, can't you dress her like everyone else?"

My parents listened attentively, nodding now and then. "But *we* don't dress her," my mother said.

"You know what I mean," the woman said. "Get her normal clothes."

"And what are normal clothes?"

"You know, you *know*! Look around, see what the other kids wear."

"But her nonna sends her these clothes from Italy. It gives her pleasure. You want us to deny her old nonna that pleasure?"

"Whatever!" the mother said. "Just do *something*! It's driving me crazy, and I'm not the only one who feels this way, you know."

"Oh?"

"If you'd listen, you'd hear," the woman said, and with that, she left.

I'd heard it all from the kitchen. My father raised his hands to the ceiling. "People are so silly in the head!" He patted my shoulder. "To me, you look perfect."

My parents said nothing more about the complaining mother, and I didn't worry about what she had said. It wasn't as if I didn't care that other kids were whining or envious; it was more that I

18

could not understand it. I could not understand why anyone would want to look like anyone else.

So, I guess the fight was inevitable.

After school on a hot, dusty day, I got off the bus with others.

"You! Gina!" a girl said. "Gypsy!" She said *gypsy* with scorn in her voice, her words doused with lemon juice.

Two of the Groube brothers, perpetually angry boys, leaped on the challenge.

"Yeah, Gina gypsy!" they taunted.

Another said, "Get me my sunglasses. Oh, she is blinding me."

The girl who had first called my name snatched the silk scarf trailing from my waist. She pulled hard, ripping it and knocking me off balance.

"What?" I said, not challenging, but calm, because I thought it was a fleeting game.

The girl leaned in close, so close that I could

19

smell her cinnamon gum. "You think you are so special."

The Groubes took up the chant. "Special gypsy! Ooh! So *special*!"

The girl slapped me on the cheek and stood in front of me, hands on her hips, daring me to take up the challenge.

"The angel in Italy—" I began.

"Ha ha! Did you hear her?" a boy said. "An angel? In Italy?"

"—would—"

"Would *what*?" the girl said.

I smoothed the fragment of the scarf at my hip. "The angel in Italy would freeze your words and let them fall like little ice chunks onto the ground."

For a few moments there was quiet, as the girl and boys absorbed that, and then the girl snarled, "Who do you think you *are*? Talking about a stupid *angel*!"

One of the Groubes looked as if he was thinking about what I'd said, trying to picture words like ice chunks falling to the ground. At his feet was gravel, and maybe because he had no words of his own and imagined the gravel as words, or maybe simply because the gravel was there, he scooped up a handful and tossed it at me.

The stones hit my forehead and arms. As I turned to walk away, the others scooped up gravel and threw it at me, with more force this time.

There was only one thing to do: summon the angel in Italy.

The next day, my father accompanied me to the principal's office, where several mothers and their children, the gravel throwers, were gathered.

"There she is!" Mrs. Groube said. She reached down to lift her son's pant leg, revealing red welts along the shins. "See what she does, that girl!"

The others pushed their children forward, displaying welts on their legs, too.

"Ah," Dad said. "Gina?"

I pushed my bangs aside so they could see the gravel cuts. I slid the sleeves of my blouse up above the elbows, disclosing more cuts.

One mother covered her mouth, shocked to see the fresh wounds.

"But *she* started it!" one of the Groube boys said, and the others chimed in, "She did, she did!"

The principal glanced around the room, nodding at each face. "Let me speak with Gina alone," she said.

Once the door was closed, the principal said, "So? Gina? I am a little surprised."

"Yes, ma'am."

"I do not believe you started it, but I am

surprised that you fought back."

I had the feeling she was secretly pleased I had defended myself, but she could not encourage fighting.

"What prompted you?" she asked.

"The angel in Italy."

"Pardon?"

"Angel Lucia. She was with me. She told me to pick up the branch, to swing it around, low, not high, so they would trip and stumble. Then she froze the words in their mouths and all they had left were little *eee eee eee* whimpers."

"Well. I see. Hmm. Angel Lucia, you say?"

"Yes, ma'am."

The principal nodded slowly. "I could use an angel like that."

THE PORCUPINE, THE ANGELS, AND THE COUNSELOR

~

B ut after all that, after the Groubes had moved away and the new, quiet neighbors had been there about a week, I spotted Antonio standing in the middle of our backyard.

"Lose something?" I asked.

"Just checking," he said, with a ridiculously charming smile. "There was a porcupine here—right here—eating licorice."

"A porcupine? Licorice?"

"Yes, right here. It was the red kind—not the

porcupine, the licorice—you know those sticky whippy things?"

We studied the grass, turned all around. Nothing. No porcupine. No licorice bits.

"When I was little," Antonio said, "people said I had a lively imagination. Lately, though, people wonder what is wrong with me because apparently I see things that others do not." A puff of disappointment left his mouth.

"People have said that about me, too," I admitted.

"They have?" He nodded appreciatively. "That's good to know." As he turned away, he said, "Gotta go. Let me know if you see any porcupines—"

"Or licorice," I said. "I'll let you know."

When I told Dad about Antonio and the porcupine, he reminded me of another encounter I'd had at school a few years earlier. From the window of my classroom I had seen two angels sitting in a tree. They were whispering to each other and their wings were folded against their backs and thin gold halos hovered above their heads. They saw me and I saw them. One of them waved shyly. I waved back.

"Gina?" my teacher said. "Gina! This world is waiting for you! Hello, hello?"

I mentioned the angels whispering in the tree. "See? There?"

The teacher and my classmates turned toward the window, peering at the lone tree at the edge of the playground. Then they turned to peer at me. I knew that look. They did not see the angels. They thought I was lying.

My teacher phoned my parents and asked for a conference.

After the conference, my mother took me to an eye doctor to have my vision checked (my father didn't think it was necessary), and at school a counselor asked me many, many questions. He wanted to know, for example, if anyone was bullying me.

"Of course," I said.

"'Of course'? Is it someone in your class?"

"No."

"At home?"

"No."

"Then where?"

I tapped my head. "Here."

"Ah," he said, adding a little star by my response. I thought maybe the star meant I'd said something especially good. Then he asked if I'd ever been locked in a room or closet.

"Maybe."

"Maybe? You don't know for sure?"

"In which world?"

"Pardon?"

"Well, do you mean this world here, or other

worlds, like in a movie or in my mind?"

He wrote down some more words and added several stars.

Next we examined splatters of black ink on white paper, and he asked what I saw there.

"Splatters of black ink," I said.

"Well, yes, but what do the splatters look like?"

"They look like someone spilled an ink bottle on the paper. Maybe they were using one of those pens that you dip in ink, and then maybe they sneezed or something and then the bottle spilled all over the paper and it was a big mess."

"Erm, yes. How about this one? Does it resemble anything? What does it remind you of?"

"It reminds me of the other one with the spilled ink."

"But does it resemble, oh, say, a butterfly? Or a bird? Or a dragon?"

"Is that what *you* see?" I asked.

"Well, yes, this one here reminds me of a fierce dragon with open mouth, but you might see something different, of course."

I figured this was a trick. If I squinted at the splatters, I could envision many elaborate scenes: a winged hero, an injured dog, erupting volcanoes, but I thought that if I said so, the counselor would think I was childish.

I said, "Do you often have those visions—of butterflies or birds or dragons?"

The counselor scratched his wrist and cleared his throat. "I don't," he started, "erm, these aren't, I was merely suggesting that others often think these—these ink blots—resemble, oh, various other things." He stared at his shoes, tapping the toes against the carpet. On his tablet, he made some jagged squiggle marks.

The counselor informed my parents and my teachers that perhaps I was "simply a child with an overactive imagination. *Very* overactive."

Dad told me that if I ever saw those angels again when I was at school maybe I should just keep it to myself. "But if you see them here at home," he said, "let me know. I'd like to see them, too."

THE NEW TEACHER

～⌒

Disappointed:

Antonio was not at the bus stop on the first day of school. Maybe he was being homeschooled or attending a private school and there would be even fewer chances to see him.

Relieved:

My homeroom teacher, soft-spoken Miss Lightstone, was new to the school and would not be aware of the incident with the angels, and she definitely did not seem like my previous year's teacher. Maybe I could have a fresh start.

My previous year's teacher was pointy—all sharp angles and shrill voice. She did not seem to like us students and she especially did not like anything I wrote. My handwriting was "messy," my sentences "awkward," my spelling "unacceptable," and when we did a unit on creative writing, she wrote at the top of one paper, *What is this supposed to be?* and on another, *Try again!* and on others, *Read the directions and do over.*

I was relieved that she no longer worked at our school.

The new teacher, Miss Lightstone, was the English language arts teacher. On the board on the first morning, she had written her name and these words: *Who are you?* With one finger she underlined the words *Who are you?*

She was probably wondering about each of us, about who we were, but I was wondering—and maybe we all were—the same about her.

At the end of the day, Miss Lightstone returned to the board and again traced beneath the words *Who are you?* She turned to us and said, "What an interesting year this will be."

On the bus on the way home, I sat with my friends. One of them, Margie, was agitated.

"But what does it *mean?* Why did she underline that question with her finger like that? Are we supposed to answer her question about who we are?"

Arif, sitting across the aisle, said, "Do you think it's a test? Maybe tomorrow we will have to write an essay on who we are." He drummed restlessly on the seat in front of him. "What should we say? Who *are* we?"

Margie pulled on my arm. "Are we supposed to know?"

While I had been in class, I liked not knowing why that question was on the board. I liked wondering about it. But now, listening to Margie and Arif, I started worrying. Were we supposed to be prepared for something tomorrow? I didn't like being unprepared.

Sometimes my mother would say *"Shiyou ga nai"* when one of us was faced with something we couldn't help or change. "So why worry? *Shiyou ga nai.* What can you do?"

I once asked her where she learned that foreign phrase, but it was my father who answered.

"She used to have a Japanese boyfriend."

My mother batted at him with a dish towel. "You jealous?"

My father said, "No. *Shiyou ga nai.*"

MARGIE AND ARIF AND RENALDO AND FREDDY AND ME

❧

Arif and Margie were the two students I clumped with most of the time. We weren't tightly bonded but felt natural together. We weren't like the strutting, confident ones or like the rough, loud ones or like the squeamish ones. We were just us.

Arif was a slight boy with long arms and delicate hands and golden eyes. When he was nervous, he tapped the sides of his legs or kicked absently at the seat in front of him. Each day before homeroom began, he stood in front of the board with his arms crossed and one foot kicking absently at the baseboard. He leaned in close, his nose nearly touching *Who are you?*

Margie, who sat in front of me, often rested her elbows on her desk, chin in her hands, head swiveling left, right and center. Each time her head turned, mine followed, not wanting to miss anything. Like Arif, she often fidgeted, chewing her nails or pulling on a strand of hair, and also like Arif, she was particularly curious about *Who are you?*

I was a skinny-legged and skinny-armed girl, with a mass of dark, thick hair—not curly exactly, but wavy and tangled. I think I was the only one in my class who had no brothers or sisters, and I envied those who did. My default mode was watching and listening and daydreaming and trying to slow my jumbled brain. When other kids spoke, their words seemed to float in the air, but I felt that when I talked, my words sank like stones, except when I was with Arif and Margie.

Who are you?

One day Margie asked Miss Lightstone if there was a right answer to that question.

"No," Miss Lightstone said. "There is no right answer."

"Is there a wrong answer?"

"I don't think so, Margie. What do you think, Arif?"

Arif curled into himself. "Me? You're asking *me*?"

"Or anyone," Miss Lightstone said, glancing around the room. "What do you think?"

Renaldo's hand shot into the air. "I know! I know!"

We all cringed, expecting one of Renaldo's goofy jokes.

"And what is that?" Miss Lightstone said.

We all braced for the worst, for the dumbest joke, the most inappropriate answer.

"Maybe the answer is different every day."

A few people groaned. Most of us turned to Miss Lightstone, to see what her reaction would be.

"Interesting possibility, Renaldo. What do you think, class?"

We all nodded dumbly, like a slew of bobbing frogs.

You could sense brains melting all over the room, partly at the suggestion that we might be different each day, but also because that was probably the first time we'd seen Renaldo so openly praised. He was so often joking and playing pranks that we didn't take him seriously.

And then there was Freddy, the class cynic. Nothing impressed him. Nothing fully interested him. "Who cares?" he often said. "Who really cares?"

While I was wondering how I would answer the question about who I was, Freddy said, "Who cares? I don't see what the big deal is. I mean who really cares?"

MISS LIGHTSTONE

Miss Lightstone was young and petite, with wild, unruly red hair. She had large, sparkly, hazel eyes and long, pale eyelashes. Her clothing was a colorful mix of yellow and orange or red and bright blue. Her lipstick was raspberry colored.

At first I did not know what to make of her. She did not begin with rules. Instead she asked us to help her sort books, and in the middle of that, she stopped to read the beginning of one.

"Oh, this one is a favorite," she said. "I'll just read the first page." Her voice took on a different tone, one that we would soon recognize as her reading voice—a fluid, resonant, rich tone. When she stopped, the room was silent. She looked up from the page. "What? You want more? Maybe later."

While we sorted and stacked books that morning, she frequently stopped to read from another "favorite"—sometimes it was a poem, sometimes a chilling opening paragraph, sometimes a humorous passage.

I was hypnotized. I'd only ever heard my parents read aloud to me, and it had been a few years since they had done so. My mother read so rapidly that my brain was always a few paragraphs behind. My father was blessed with many virtues, but reading aloud was not one of them, for he stumbled over long words and used the same voice for every character.

But Miss Lightstone was a master. By the end of the first week, she had us in the palm of her hand.

Well, most of us.

"What's the big deal with the reading?" Freddy said. "Reading schmeading. I don't have time for it."

FIRST LINES

One morning when we entered the classroom there were three or four books on each desk. Renaldo held one aloft. "This is way too hard. Anyone want to trade?"

"Wait," Miss Lightstone said. "Wait a leetle min-oo-toe."

She asked us to leaf through the books on our desks and to read the opening line of each (silently, to ourselves), and then to write down the one opening that most appealed to us. Then we were to pass the books to the person on our right and receive the books from the person at our left, and repeat the process of choosing the best first line, until we'd seen all the books.

So many books, each so different.

It was surprising how one sentence—the first sentence—of a book had the power to draw you in or push you back, but not everyone was drawn in or pushed back by the same sentence. We discovered this when we each read aloud our favorite openers.

"Makes you wonder what will happen."

"Ugh. Bor-ing."

"Sounds gooey, like it was meant for little kids."

"The sounds of the words are hypnotizing."

We each chose a line to add to the bulletin board.

Margie whispered to me, "Why do you think we are putting them on the board? Do you think it will be a test or something?"

Freddy said, "Who cares?"

THE BLUE FROG

~

One afternoon, as I was walking back from the bus stop, dodging a band of Clackerty-Claffertys who had jumped off the bus in a noisy heap, I spotted Antonio standing in our driveway. I hadn't seen him in nearly a week. There he was, that smile on his face. My own smile, I thought, must be inferior by comparison.

I think it matters how people look at you when they first see you, before they have a chance to rearrange their expression.

"Do you need help?" I asked.

"Why do you keep asking me that?"

"No reason."

He asked me to tell him about the bus. "Does it take you right to the school or does it stop at other places?"

"It stops to pick up other students and then it goes right to the school. Are you going to be taking the bus?"

His curly black hair hung down over one side of his forehead. When I'd ask him a question, he'd pull at one of those forehead locks, thinking.

"That may be," he said.

"I can show you how it works, if you want."

"Saw a tiny blue frog in the street today," he said.

"You did? A blue frog?"

"A man came along and ate it."

"The man ate the blue frog?"

"Yes, and then he croaked."

From the upstairs window the grandmother called, "Ann-tone-ee-oh!"

"You sure you don't need help?"

"Quit asking me that. Gotta go."

I went in my house and ate toast and wondered who had croaked, the frog or the man?

WHO IS IT?

At the beginning and end of each day, Miss Lightstone would silently trace her finger below *Who are you?* and then turn to look at each of us with a slow, roving gaze.

"I still think it's going to be a test," Margie said.

"A test?" Arif asked. "How could it be a test?"

"Like maybe an essay test," Margie said. "Maybe we're supposed to be thinking about it and preparing to answer that question."

I did not like the sound of that, but the idea lodged in my head like an annoying fly. *Figure it out. Who* are *you? What is the answer? What will you say?*

One morning, there was a word in bold writing pinned on the bulletin board: **reflection**.

Nearby was a photo of a still lake with trees on the bank perfectly reflected in the water. Beneath the photo were the words *Green Lake*.

While we were contemplating these new additions, Margie said, "Well, they're connected—there's a *reflection* in the photo of Green Lake."

"A lake that isn't there," Freddy said.

"What are you talking about?" Arif asked. "The lake is right there."

Freddy approached the board and jabbed his finger at one of the first lines we had posted on the day we examined piles of books: "There is no lake at Camp Green Lake."[1]

"Wait—what?"

"It's a test, I know it."

Renaldo, who was standing to one side, said, "Who's that?"

Miss Lightstone was now at the classroom door speaking with the office secretary, Miss Judy, who handed our teacher a folder. A student stood beside her, but we couldn't tell if it was a boy or a girl. We could only see an arm and a leg.

---

1. *Holes*, Louis Sachar.

MISS JUDY AND MISS MARLENE

 ⌒

The previous day, we had read aloud short passages of dialogue from several different books, taking turns as the characters. We sounded as if we were in miniature plays: people didn't always talk in complete sentences, often they interrupted each other, and sometimes they talked over each other.

Afterward, we did a writing experiment: a conversation between two people. It could be a real conversation or a made-up one.

I wrote about the time Dad and I visited two older women who used to work at the university where he taught part-time. One of the women, Miss Judy, I knew because she now worked in the office at our school. She and her friend Miss Marlene were slender and frail, birdlike in their jittery movements. They served us tea and cookies and talked over each other:

Miss Judy:	(*pointing to Dad's chair*) Do you know who sat in that chair—
Miss Marlene:	—the one you're sitting in—
Miss Judy:	The empress of Japan!
Miss Marlene:	Right there!
Miss Judy:	At this table, only it wasn't this table—
Miss Marlene:	This table wasn't fancy enough—
Miss Judy:	So we had to cart up a different table—

Miss Marlene:	And we made tea in these little cups—
Miss Judy:	These same cups you're drinking out of—
Miss Marlene:	And we had little cookies—
Miss Judy:	Better than these cookies—we had little fancy ones—
Miss Marlene:	For the empress of Japan—
Miss Judy:	And we're talking, talking—
Miss Marlene:	Talking, talking—
Miss Judy:	And after all this talking, do you know what the empress of Japan said?
Miss Marlene:	It was so—so—cute.
Miss Judy:	She said, "May I have a cookie?"
Miss Marlene:	The empress of Japan!
Miss Judy:	"May I have a cookie?"

They were so eager, Miss Judy and Miss Marlene, to tell us their story of the visit of the empress of Japan, and when they finished, Dad nodded appreciatively while I looked longingly at the cookies.

Because Miss Judy worked in our school office, I saw her nearly every day. She winked at me, even if I was late or in trouble, like the time when I saw the angels.

Now, Miss Judy was standing like a gawky bird in the doorway of our classroom, handing Miss Lightstone a folder and introducing her to a new student. The whir this set off in our class reminded me of sitting with Miss Judy and Miss Marlene and hearing the tale of the empress of Japan. There was a rhythm to the whispers in my class, and I tried to capture it quickly in my notebook.

Who is that?

Is it a boy? Is he new?

Must be—

Never seen him—

Or her. Maybe it's a girl.

Will he—or she—be—

In our class—

Oh, I hope so—

What's the big deal?

Who is it?

Starting school two weeks late?

Must have just moved here—

From where?

Who is it?

"Class," Miss Lightstone said, ushering a boy into the room, "we have a new student. This is Antonio."

Everyone gaped at him. He was so perfectly

perfect standing there, confident and at ease, all cleaned up.

He smiled.

At *everyone*.

THE NEW BOY

~

My classmates tripped all over themselves offering to help "the new boy," volunteering to show Antonio around the school and where to put his jacket and how to maneuver the cafeteria line and how to interpret the schedule and, honestly, I think they would have taught him how to walk and talk if he had needed it.

"He's so different—"

"Mysterious—"

"Do you see how he smiles?"

Yes, I saw how he smiled, and I was disappointed.

He was in our room for nearly ten minutes before he recognized me.

"Hey," he said. "This your class?"

"Yep."

And then someone nudged him, eager to show him something, and he turned away.

Margie snagged my arm. "You *know* him? How do you *know* him?" She sounded as if she were accusing me of keeping him a secret.

"Neighbor," I said, watching him being ushered across the room by Arif and Renaldo, with Claire, Audrey, and Ruby trailing behind.

Margie was affronted. "You never said! You never mentioned him!"

"He hasn't been here long."

Miss Lightstone seated him at the one empty desk on the far side of the room, near the bulletin board. Just before lunch, Audrey asked Miss

Lightstone if Antonio could sit near her, because she was "very good at helping new people." Ruby said that she, too, was very good at helping new people.

Antonio seemed dazed by all the attention, but not so dazed that he forgot to smile. He offered everyone the gift of that smile, everyone in equal measure.

I was feeling grouchy about that, but when the dismissal bell rang at the end of the day, Antonio made a point of finding me and asking me if I would show him where to catch the bus.

"Sure," I said, aware that other students—Margie and Audrey and Claire and Ruby especially—were surprised, momentarily frozen in place.

He joined me in the bus line and he sat beside me on the bus.

That was no small thing.

Normally, I sat with Margie or one of the

other girls. Boys and girls did not usually sit together, and I briefly worried that other boys would make fun of him, but they did not.

He told me he didn't want to get off at the wrong stop.

The next morning, he waited in his driveway until I came out of my house, and we walked to the bus stop together.

He sat beside me on the bus.

When we reached school, he said, "Okay, now I know how to do it."

Renaldo greeted him and then a few other students joined them and they all walked into school together and that was the last day Antonio sat beside me on the bus or waited for me in the morning.

THE SMILE

~

A person was more than a smile. I knew that.

I knew that, and still I was mesmerized by Antonio's smile—the way it began slowly and then got wider and wider—and I attributed all sorts of positive things to his character because of that smile.

He must be a good person.

He must be happy.

He must be kind.

He must be thoughtful.

He must be smart.

He must like me.

He didn't smile *all* the time, or else he would have appeared goofy, like Renaldo. Sometimes Renaldo was funny and sometimes not, but if I was around him too much, I got a headache.

I did not get a headache around Antonio.

THE MOON AND THE LAKE

On the bulletin board, a new word: **lunar**.

Beside the word: a photo of a creamy full moon against a dark sky, reflected in a lake below.

Beneath the word and the photo, a new *first line*: "Rendi was not sure how long the moon had been missing."[2]

"*Lunar* refers to the moon," Margie said.

---

2. *Starry River of the Sky*, Grace Lin.

"Everyone knows that," Freddy felt compelled to add.

Arif studied the board. "And the moon is in the photo."

"And the moon," Renaldo added, "is in that first line of a book."

Freddy approached the board. "Except that in the book the moon is *missing*: 'Rendi was not sure how long *the moon had been missing.*'"

Like me, Antonio was watching and listening, but said nothing.

Midway through attendance-taking, Margie jumped up. "That new image with the moon— see? It's also a *reflection*—just like the other picture with the trees and the lake." She sat down, cradling her head in her hands. "What does it all mean?"

Renaldo adopted a stern voice and demanded, "Who put it there?" He drummed his fingers loudly on his desk. "Did you, Miss Lightstone?"

She raised her eyes from the attendance book, blinked a few times, glanced at the board, and murmured, "Hmm."

The rest of the day was a blur of books and assignments and in the midst of it all, an awareness that Antonio was accumulating fans, layers of students surrounding him wherever he went.

At dismissal, he was whisked aboard the bus by several boys and they all sat in the back, talking and laughing like a band of chattering crows.

It wasn't until I got off the bus that I remembered we were expecting company that day.

UNCLE AND AUNTIE PASTA

Each September, my father's aunt and uncle made a pilgrimage from New York to our home in Ohio. With them, they brought the auntie's sour mood and the ingredients to make the uncle's pasta, which he could not live without. He would not eat "store bought"—it had to be fresh—and because of their pasta obsession we privately referred to them as Uncle and Auntie Pasta.

They also brought two presents for me. The presents were always the same: a pair of white socks with lacy cuffs (the sort of socks I wore when I was four) and a contribution to the money box they had given me when I was born. The money box was a square tin painted with red and yellow flowers. In the top was a narrow slot. During each visit, Uncle Pasta would make a great show of presenting me with a coin to put in the box. When I was little, it was a nickel. Later, a dime. Then a quarter.

"Save, save, save!" Uncle Pasta ordered as he handed me the coin each year.

One time after they'd left, Mom said, "Maybe by the time you are all grown up, you can buy yourself a cup of coffee with those savings."

To prepare for the visits from the auntie and uncle, I cleared space in my dresser and closet so they could have my room, and I slept on a cot in the hall.

"The bed, it is too small," the auntie complained.

"Too lumpy, oh, my back," moaned the uncle.

My mother conveniently had to work late most nights that the auntie and uncle were in town.

The auntie made pasta for lunch and dinner, for this was all the uncle would eat, and it is what the rest of us ate, too. Flour littered the counters; sauce splattered the stove and floor.

"You need to learn to make pasta," the auntie told me, but when I offered to help, the auntie said, "No, no, *I* make this. Uncle only likes *my* pasta."

When the auntie and uncle were not making or eating pasta, they liked to *visit*. "Let's *visit* a while. Talk. Catch up."

First they would tell Dad that he needed to get some help raising the *povera ragazza* (me). "If your wife has to work so much, you can't do this on your own," they told him. "You need some help. You need someone to teach her things."

The little veins on the side of Dad's neck bulged, but he did not argue. Instead, he nodded and murmured, "Mm, mm."

Auntie said, "Her head is filled with those angel stories. Tell her about the bad things, too. So many bad things!"

"Terrible, terrible," Uncle Pasta agreed.

"Our neighbor in New York, that woman, you know, I told you last time? That woman with the dogs? Shot! Outside her own apartment!"

"Shot!" Uncle Pasta echoed.

"And my cousin Guadalupe? You remember her? The one with the big nose? Cancer! From eating canned soup."

One morning, when Auntie Pasta spotted Antonio's grandmother outside, she dragged Dad to the window.

"See there? Who is that woman?"

"A grandmother. She's new here."

Auntie marched outside and spoke to the

grandmother, while Dad and I stayed at the window watching. Antonio's grandmother stood very still, listening to Auntie Pasta, whose arms waved in the air, occasionally pointing toward our house.

Auntie returned triumphant. "I fix it!" she said.

"Fix *what*?" Dad asked.

"I told her about you and *povera* Gina, with her mother working so much and you needing some help."

Dad was not amused. "You *what*?"

"I will fix. You'll see."

They tried so hard, Auntie and Uncle Pasta, and I knew they meant well, but when they left, I stood on the front steps waving at the back end of their car, relieved.

MÅNGATA

~

One morning at school Renaldo raced into class waving a blue notecard. "I have a great word! Wait till you see!"

He showed Miss Lightstone the card. "Really?" she said.

"Really. My grandpa is Swedish."

"Okay, then, go ahead."

Renaldo tacked the card next to the word *lunar* and the picture of the moon's reflection in the water. Reading from the card, he said,

"*Mångata*, a Swedish word meaning the path-like reflection of the moon over water." He touched the photo of the moon already on the board. "See? That light path that the moon makes in the water? That reflection? That's *mångata*."

I rolled the word around in my mouth: *man-gotta, MAN-gotta*. It amazed me that there was a single word to describe the way the moon's light reflects on a body of water, creating a path, as if inviting you to follow it back to the moon.

Miss Lightstone ran her hands through her hair. "Words!"

Others chimed in:

"*Mångata!*"

"Mooooon!"

"Lunar!"

"Re-flec-tion!"

"Stupid!"

That last one was Freddy, pouring cold water on our enthusiasm. Was there a word for doing just that, spoiling the mood with one word? Maybe it would be *floshenslosh* or *splattenmatt*.

Audrey and Ruby hovered beside Antonio's desk.

"Ooh, *mångata*! Isn't that funny, Antonio?"

"Isn't it so—so—unusual and—and—"

"Particular? Specific?" he added.

"Oh, yes! That's it, Antonio! It's so—so—particular and specific!"

I caught his eye for a moment and must have blinked my annoyance, for he turned his palms up as if to say it wasn't his fault. What was he to do, poor, innocent, Antonio?

Ugh.

When I got home that day, Dad was already there, standing in the kitchen.

"Toast," I said. "I need toast, with buckets of butter and cinnamon and sugar."

"That makes two of us. Take a look at this."

On the counter were several serving bowls covered with foil. "You'll never guess who stopped by."

"Who?"

Dad nodded toward Antonio's house. "Her. That lady. That grandmother."

"No."

"Yes. She brought us food. Auntie Pasta told her about *povera* you, without someone to make—"

"No, no. Don't tell me. No. Is it—I bet it's—"

He nodded sadly, a defeated man, and lifted the foil. "Pasta: Ravioli! Spaghetti and meatballs! Cavatelli!"

SHEEP TALK AND FAMILY TREES

❧

One time after school, when I had nearly reached my house, Antonio called out to me. He had hopped off the bus as usual with a posse of kids and had stood there chatting with them while I kept walking. Now, he caught up to me.

"I saw the sheep today," he said.

"What sheep?"

"Two sheep, gray and dirty. They were having

a conversation. I tried to tell Arif and Renaldo about them, but they didn't believe me."

"What were the sheep talking about?"

"Family trees."

"Really? Odd subject for sheep, don't you think?"

He stuffed his hands in his pockets. "No. Why shouldn't they talk about family trees?"

"Sticky subject," I said.

Later, I told my parents about Antonio seeing the two sheep, gray and dirty, having a conversation. "He told some other kids about the sheep, but they didn't believe him."

My mother said, "The sheep were having a conversation?"

"Yes, and you know what they were talking about? Family trees."

My parents exchanged a glance. Dad said,

"Uh-oh. Sticky subject, Gina."

"That's exactly what I said."

One time the previous year's pointy teacher said we were going to create family trees, and using her own family as an example, she created her family tree on the board. She wrote the names of each of her great-grandparents, grandparents and parents, along with her siblings and with her own name at the bottom. Her name looked so important there, with all those people merging to create her.

For homework she gave us a printout with blank spaces on branches so we could fill in the names of our own family members and ancestors.

From the start, it did not go well. We had questions.

"What if you have two mothers?"

"Or two fathers?"

"How can you have two mothers or two fathers?"

"Or if one is dead?"

"Or both, what if they're both dead?"

"Or if they're divorced?"

"Or no father?"

"How can you have no father?"

The pointy teacher said, "Ask your parents. They'll know what you should write."

But many of the parents did not know what to write. It was surprising how many versions of trees there could be.

Some parents were angry and complained.

"This is no business of the school's."

"We refuse to submit this."

"My husband was very upset by this."

"Some of us might be adopted, you know. Which parents and grandparents do you want on this form?"

The following evening, a previously scheduled parent meeting to review policies and upcoming events erupted into a loud, messy complaint session when several parents raised the issue of the family trees.

Mom was working that night, but Dad, who dreaded going to such meetings, went because he felt obligated. On that evening, he came home and said, "Toast! I need toast. People are so angry and crazy!"

The next day the pointy teacher canceled the family tree assignment. Many students were relieved, some were merely puzzled, but a few were frustrated and angry.

"What? I spent five hours on my tree. Five hours! And you're going to cancel it?"

"Can I get credit for the one I already finished? It's not fair if those of us who did them don't get credit while the ones who didn't do anything get away with being lazy."

"I wasn't lazy! My dad forbid me!"

On and on it went. It took weeks for people to settle down.

And then, a year later, came the day that Miss Lightstone unknowingly stepped into that old swamp.

THAT OLD SWAMP

 ~

It was at the end of class one day, after we'd been talking about characters in a book and how they were related to each other, that Miss Lightstone announced that it might be interesting to work on our own family trees.

Around the room came a collective groan, followed by:

"Ack!"

"No!"

"Please no!"

Arif raised a hand. "Not to be rude, Miss Lightstone, but in this school, we don't talk about family trees."

"You don't?" She put a finger to her raspberry lips. "Hmm. Interesting." She walked slowly around the room, studying each of us. "Hmm." When she reached the front of the room again, she said, "As you know, I am new here, and therefore it may take me some time to learn— about—about—this school's—erm—*traditions*."

She stopped in front of the *Who are you?* written on the board.

"Would anyone like to tell me why the family trees are so . . . so . . . problematic?"

Some students looked down at their desks or bent to tie their shoes or anything to avoid her direct gaze. Others turned to Arif and Renaldo, the two most likely to speak up, but it was Margie who raised her hand.

"It's complicated, Miss Lightstone, and it's

sensitive. Many parents object."

Arif added, "Many get very, very angry."

Others then chimed in:

"My dad said it's too intrusive."

"Like what if we didn't have a father or a mother or—"

"If we had two fathers or three or—"

"If we were adopted or—"

Audrey and Ruby were crying.

Miss Lightstone held up both hands. "I see, I see. It's okay." Her quiet, reassuring voice was like a warm embrace. "I understand. We will not be doing family trees."

Antonio was following all this with great interest, sitting straighter and straighter in his chair until it looked as if he might lift off and float to the ceiling. His hand rose into the air.

"I have an idea," he said. "What if we do fictional family trees, you know, like make up our ancestors?"

"Make them up?" Miss Lightstone said.

"You can't just go making up your ancestors!" Freddy said.

"I mean, for fun," Antonio said. "Like if you imagined who you might *want* your ancestors to be, like, say, a king or queen or—or—pirate—"

Others chimed in immediately.

"Or basketball star—"

"Or president—"

"Or writer—"

"Or painter—"

"And then," Arif suggested, "you could imagine who *you* might be if you had those ancestors, right?"

Miss Lightstone stood in front of the board and let her finger trace, again, under the words *Who are you?* and then she wrote another question below it: *Who would you be?*

She stood back and considered what she had written, and then she erased the word *would* and wrote *could* in its place: *Who **could** you be?*

Little brain cells collided in my head. Who *could* I be? It felt daring and revolutionary.

Arif slapped at his head as if his hair were on fire. "Wow! That is—wow!"

Renaldo looked wary, almost frightened, but then his expression changed and he grinned. "Yes!" he shouted. "Perfecto!"

Freddy said, "Stupid idea."

PASTA AND THE FRAILS

~⌒~

"All this pasta!" Dad exclaimed one Saturday morning. "We've eaten some, frozen some, and still—so much left." He pulled a few bowls from the refrigerator. "Come on, we're going to visit the Frails."

"The Frails" was Dad's affectionate nickname for Miss Judy and Miss Marlene, the school secretary and her friend who had once entertained the empress of Japan with cookies and tea.

"Those Frails need some meat on their bones," Dad said.

I was used to seeing Miss Judy at school, either in the office or hallways, and although she was thin, I didn't think of her as frail because she always seemed so energetic. She would stride purposefully down the halls, swinging one arm as she balanced a stack of books or papers in the other arm. She had a cheerful greeting for all, and sometimes from our classroom you could hear her going by, calling out "Hello!" and "Howdy!" and "Beautiful!" and "Ciao!" and "Ta-da!"

Miss Judy and Miss Marlene were so happy with our pasta offerings that you might have thought we'd offered them a bowl of expensive chocolates. As they spoke, I imagined how their dialogue would appear on the page.

"How delightful!"

"Mmm, and it smells so very—"

"Delicious!"

"Scrumptious!"

"Delectable!"

"Did you make—"

"This yourselves?"

Miss Marlene and Miss Judy insisted that we stay for tea and—

"Cookies!"

"You'll have cookies!"

"Like the empress of Japan!"

The hallway between the kitchen and the living room was covered with framed photographs that I hadn't paid attention to before, but this time, as they were talking with Dad, I studied them. There were photos of young people and old people, of couples and families, of small groups and large. There were new babies and kids learning to ride bikes and to swim and older teens in graduation gowns. There was a teenage Miss Marlene on a sailboat and a young Miss

Judy hugging a goat and photos of both of them at protest rallies.

How much life they must have seen. When they were young, what did they think and what did they see and what did they feel?

As we were leaving, Miss Judy placed a bony but strangely beautiful, almost translucent hand on my arm. She leaned in close and whispered, "Did I hear that Miss Lightstone assigned family trees? I do hope she will be careful."

"It's okay. We're doing fictional ones, not real ones."

"Fictional family trees? How can you—?"

"You know, like for characters in books—not for real, no, no, not for real."

Miss Judy considered this. "I do hope she is careful."

A PACKAGE

~∂~

Back at home that same day, I was filling the bird feeders when Antonio's cousin Carlotta opened their back door to let out the cranky cat, Mr. Blue. I had seen neither Mr. Blue nor Carlotta for weeks and was beginning to think they no longer lived there.

Carlotta was a sturdy girl, tall and muscled, and although it was warm out, she wore a knit hat pulled down over her hair, sweatpants and a baggy sweatshirt. Antonio had said she was taking a semester off from college.

"Hey," I said, offering a wave.

She turned her head in my direction, gave me a slow nod and backed into the house, leaving Mr. Blue squatting on the parsley plants staring menacingly, warning me to stay away.

The postman came up the drive with a package. "For you, Miss Gina Filomena," he said. He always called me that, formally, as if I were a person of some status.

The package, from Nonna Filomena, contained a letter addressed to all of us and, wrapped in pale yellow tissue paper, a delicate, gauzy black scarf embroidered with dozens of multicolored flowers joined by sinuous green vines. It smelled slightly of roses.

I draped it around my neck and studied my reflection in the hall mirror. I felt transformed, as I often did when receiving these colorful gifts.

They were imbued with lively sparks, filled with angel air.

Dad, translating, read from her letter:

I am thinking of you day and night and beaming you bushels of love and all good things.

I hope, Gina, that you will treasure this scarf. Each tiny flower I embroidered with my own old hands.

As Dad traced along a vine, he returned to the letter and translated the latest Angel Lucia news:

There was a mean man who was always in the local park shaking his cane at the children running and playing, and he sometimes hit the dogs as they ran past, and he spit on the sidewalk, too.

One time Angel Lucia placed a puppy at his feet, and the puppy had big sad eyes and sat on the man's shoes until the man picked him up. The puppy licked the man's face and the man cried and the children asked him what was wrong and the other dogs came to sniff the new puppy.

And now, you know what, Gina? The children and the other dogs look forward to the arrival of the man with the puppy, and the man no longer shakes his cane or hits the other dogs or spits on the sidewalk.

THE WORLD TURNS

~⌒~

By late October, the bulletin boards were filling up with words and images and first lines.
Whenever any of us came across an interesting or puzzling word in our reading, we put it
on the board, where they now formed a word-
world of their own:

lunar	reflection	*mångata*
quantum	aggressive	passive
translucent	formidable	Neanderthal

harridan	sinister	perspicacious
trompe l'oeil	precipice	cascade
deluge	sinuous	resonate
affirmation	confirmation	

. . . and dozens more.

One day even Freddy—scornful of so many things—proudly attached a word to the board: *komorebi*.

"It's a word from my grandfather," he explained, as he also attached a photograph of a tree-lined street. "See the way the sun comes through the leaves? That filtered light coming through—that's *komorebi*."

There was a single word for that?

Renaldo clapped. "Bravo, Freddy! That is a great word. *Komorebi, komorebi, komorebi!*"

The rest of us took up the chant: "*Komorebi, komorebi, komorebi!*"

Freddy blushed, permitting a brief smile to

acknowledge the praise.

The images on the board now included magazine pictures, photographs, and drawings. There were majestic landscapes and eerie ones, unusual animals and adorable ones, and people of all shapes and sizes and colors.

The first lines from twenty or thirty books formed a long column on the adjacent board. The lines that most jumped out at me were:

"There is no lake at Camp Green Lake."

"Rendi was not sure how long the moon had been missing."

"In a hole in the ground there lived a hobbit."[3]

"We didn't always live on Mango Street."[4]

"We think they took my papi."[5]

"My name is Elizabeth but no one's ever called me that."[6]

---

3. *The Hobbit*, J. R. R. Tolkien.
4. *The House on Mango Street*, Sandra Cisneros.
5. *Harbor Me*, Jacqueline Woodson.
6. *How I Live Now*, Meg Rosoff.

One day, Margie turned to me and said, "Something is growing there," and I agreed that yes, something was indeed growing there, but I was not sure *what*.

One morning as we entered class, Antonio, who was flanked by his growing posse, stopped abruptly, put his hands out as if to steady himself, and said, "Whoa! Feel that?"

"What?"

"Feel what?"

Antonio momentarily swayed. "Isn't that amazing?"

"What?"

"*What* is amazing?"

"Didn't you feel that?"

"Um . . ."

Antonio looked baffled. "No? Really?" He continued on his way to his seat. "Sometimes, you can feel the earth turning."

I think that was the first day I noticed a few kids distance themselves from Antonio, as if some of his charm was fading or that he was deemed a bit odd. He still had many admirers, though, far outnumbering those few who now held back.

As for me, I was increasingly mesmerized by him, but I was silent and cautious, watching and listening. I felt as if we were both vulnerable, maybe in the way that I was vulnerable to the taunts and attacks of the Groube brothers and others when I was young. I hadn't understood then that what I said or what I wore could be a source of irritation to others. Besides, I had felt I had Angel Lucia's protection.

Now I was aware of that vulnerability and was more quiet and more the observer because of it, but I worried about Antonio. I still felt that odd obligation to protect him. I wasn't even sure why.

SWIRLS

~

Words from the bulletin board swirled through my mind all day, so that out of nowhere, even in math class, words would appear, demanding attention:

Precipice! Harridan!

Deluge! Formidable!

Quantum! Lunar!

Mångata! *Komorebi!*

Sinister!

Cascade!

Artifact!

Torrential!

Images from the board appeared—altered or exaggerated or combined—in my dreams at night. There would be a lake with a hobbit jumping into it, or a street lined with mangoes, or mountains beneath the ocean, or the moon underwater.

The first lines of books jumped in and out of my dreams, begging to be knitted together, but in doing so they formed new, strange combinations:

Antonio was not sure how long the house on Mango Street had been missing.
And
There was no moon in the lake.
And
In a hole in the ground lived Gina Filomena.

One time Miss Lightstone said, "Let's write. Think of these boards as your personal well of inspiration. Pull from them whatever you like—a word, an image, a first line—and run with it."

"Run?" Audrey said.

"You have paper, pens, pencils, mm?" Miss Lightstone said. "Have some fun. Experiment."

Margie said, "I'm not exactly sure what you want us to do."

"I want you to do what *you* want to do. Does one of those images remind you of something? Do you want to write about that? Or combine some of those words? I want you to experiment."

"But," Audrey asked. "How will we be graded?"

"Ah," Miss Lightstone said. She was wearing a peach-flowered dress and when she stood by the window, the light of the dress reflected on her face. "Experiments are not graded. Begone, grades!"

Around the room, some were genuinely excited by this project, while others, like Arif and Ruby, nibbled at their fingers, unsure and wary. Margie was nodding, warming to the possibilities, and Antonio's smile was widening.

I stared at the blank page. It seemed both intimidating and inviting.

"Okay," Renaldo said. "This is cool."

"Or stupid," Freddy added.

"Freddy," Miss Lightstone said from her place at the window, "if you want, you could write about the most stupid thing on the board, or—"

"Okay, okay," Freddy said, "I get it."

We sat there fidgeting with our pencils. Which to choose? How to begin? Arif tapped at his leg, as if inspiration would spring from it. Antonio closed his eyes. My hands were sweaty as I thought about what the pointy teacher from the previous year had said about my writing.

After a few minutes of this, Miss Lightstone said, "Ah, I am sensing that perhaps there is too much choice. Sometimes that is harder than too little choice or no choice at all."

EXPERIMENT

~

As she walked among us, Miss Lightstone trailed the faintest scent of roses, reminding me of the scarf in the most recent package from Italy.

"How about this?" she said. "We'll do a mini experiment. Choose a word from the word list—any random word—and write down anything that comes to mind, maybe something the word reminds you of or something you imagine.

"Write very fast, jotting down whatever pops into your head. Don't stop to correct spelling or think. Just keep going and going, even if you have to write, 'I'm stuck, I'm stuck, I'm stuck.' I'll time you. Five minutes." She looked directly at Margie and Audrey. "This. Is. Not. Graded."

Miss Lightstone sat at her desk, with her own pencil poised. "I'll do it, too. Remember, don't stop writing. Just capture anything that pops into your head—or your pencil. Are. You. Ready? Okay, go—"

Our first attempts had mixed results. Some students were frustrated, unable to shake the strong urge to stop and erase or cross out things they had written. Some, like me, were dazed, surprised at how quickly the five minutes had passed and by how much we had written in that time and by how much of it was unexpected.

Arif waved his paper in the air. "That was crazy! There was a dangerous *precipice* and I fell off it into a black lake and I was flailing around—and then the five minutes were up. I wanted to keep going."

"Me, too, I wanted to keep going," Renaldo agreed. "I thought I was writing something funny about a *sinister* rabbit, but then it turned into something scarier. The rabbit seemed real. It was threatening me." He looked sheepish. "I know, I know, it sounds dumb, but—"

"It doesn't sound dumb," Miss Lightstone said. "It sounds intriguing."

Margie let out an audible sigh. "I kept writing 'I am stuck, stuck, stuck,' over and over until nearly the end, when suddenly *mångata* popped into my head and I saw that golden path of light on the water and then—the time was up."

Miss Lightstone was walking around the room and stopped near my desk. "Gina? It looks as if you wrote *a lot*. Do you care to comment?"

I do not normally volunteer much in class, but this time I didn't mind answering her question because I was so surprised at what had emerged. I told Miss Lightstone and the class that I'd chosen the single word *deluge*, and as soon as I started writing I felt as if there was a *deluge* of words pouring over a *precipice*, and I described the *cascade* of green water with white foam, all pouring over the *precipice* into a lake, and there was a moon overhead creating *mångata* on the water, and I wanted to follow that light path straight to the moon, and then—the time was up.

"Whoa!" Freddy said. "That was a *deluge* all right."

Antonio was staring at me. He looked at his paper and at me and back at his paper, but he didn't say anything.

We all agreed that we wanted to try the experiment again.

"As long as it's not graded, right?" Margie asked.

Miss Lightstone bowed. "Right."

Later, I was standing at the end of the lunch

line when Antonio came up behind me and poked my shoulder.

"You know that thing you wrote?" he said. "About the deluge and the precipice and the *mångata*?"

I thought he was going to mock me about it, so I didn't respond.

He said, "I saw something similar: a deluge of words pouring over a cliff into a river and above was a full moon, making that path on the water—that *mångata*—and I was just about to start down the path when the time was up. Isn't that weird? That we saw such similar things?"

"Are you making fun of me?"

"No, really, that's what I saw and what I wrote. You can read it if you want."

I didn't know what to make of it. I no longer had a deluge of words to pour forth. I think I said, merely, "Wow."

"Yeah," he said. "See ya later."

LASAGNA

~⊙

My parents stood in the middle of the kitchen, flailing their arms this way and that. "Look," Mom said. "More!" Casserole dishes and bowls lined the counter. "Lasagna, spaghetti—I can't take it! I can't eat any more pasta."

"Maybe you should say something," I suggested.

"To—?"

"To Antonio's grandmother. Tell her we can't eat all that."

"Maybe *you* should say something," Dad said.

"Oh no. I couldn't."

"I guess we'll need to visit the Frails again."

And so we did.

Miss Marlene: Oh, my!

Miss Judy: More lasagna—

Miss Marlene: And spaghetti.

  They blinked at each other.

Miss Judy: We are going to get—

Miss Marlene: So fat!

Miss Judy: But thank you!

Miss Marlene: So thoughtful!

The next day at school, when we heard Miss Judy calling out "Ciao!" and "Hello!" in the hallway, Miss Lightstone said, "That woman is so kind. Do you know what she brought the faculty today? A big pan of lasagna!"

"Lasagna?" Freddy asked. "What's that?"

"You don't know what lasagna is?" Margie said.

"Is that a crime?"

"No, I just meant—well, I thought most people would know what lasagna is."

"Well, I don't. So what is it?"

As we floundered around trying to explain lasagna, Miss Lightstone left the room and returned with a small square of lasagna on a paper plate. She displayed the sample as if it were a rare artifact.

Antonio turned to me but he didn't say anything.

Renaldo added the word *lasagna* to the board, maybe to make Freddy feel better about not having known what it was. "La-zon-ya," Renaldo said, rolling the syllables around in his mouth. "It's a cool word."

IMAGES

❧

" This time," Miss Lightstone said, "choose one of the images and immerse yourself in it. Imagine you are there. Describe what you see and hear and feel. Write fast again, see what pops up."

Audrey asked why we had to write fast. "Why can't we write slowly?"

"Because your brain moves very fast and when you follow it, you can discover intriguing connections."

"Or not," Freddy said.

"Or not," Miss Lightstone agreed. "Maybe your brain is sludge today. That's okay. Describe the sludge."

She was wearing a long, bright yellow skirt ("Do I look like a banana?" she had said when Ruby commented on its brightness), a deep purple blouse sprinkled with yellow curlicues, and orange flats. With her red hair, she seemed like a poster for radiance.

"Don't overthink it," Miss Lightstone said. "Just choose one that pops out at you."

I had thought I'd choose the moon over the water, the *mångata* image, but then another one intrigued me. It was a painting of a wide expanse of tall green grass extending far into the distance. A narrow, winding road led to the horizon. It was a quiet painting in soft greens and browns and pale blues and grays.

"Remember, you are *there*. Describe the scene.

How does it feel? What are you thinking? Why are you there? Five minutes. Fast. Ready? Go!" And off we went.

Out poured another deluge of words, easier to capture this time because I already knew the scene that I was going to describe. I wrote so fast my writing was barely legible. I imagined myself there on that winding road. The grass grew taller and taller as I walked. Soon enormous red flowers were blooming (these were not in the original painting). They dripped yellow pollen onto my head. Suddenly it was night. A white light lit up the sky. Was it the moon? Was it a pancake? A pancake?

When Miss Lightstone called "Time's up!" I stared down at my paper. What had happened there? Where had the tall red flowers come from? The nighttime light? A pancake?

Around the room, others seemed either dazed or puzzled as they reread what they had written.

"That was weird," Margie said. "My brain was humming."

"Did *I* write this?" Arif asked.

Claire pouted. "I couldn't make my brain or my hand move fast."

Miss Lightstone walked around the room. "It looks as if most of you really got into that," she said, stopping by Antonio's desk, "and had *deluges* of words. Care to comment, Antonio?"

He said he had chosen the one with the tall green grass and the winding road. "The calm one," he said, "with the pale colors, and I thought because it was a calm scene that I would be walking along there, all peaceful and content, but as I walked, enormous green stems shot into the air and were topped by velvety red blossoms and then this strange yellow light with an orange halo swept across the sky."

He turned to me. Probably my mouth was hanging open.

Freddy said, "I had barely started when my mind jumped somewhere else completely—into another painting. Is that okay?"

"Of course it's okay, Freddy," Miss Lightstone said. "It's not only okay, it's imaginative."

I had never seen Freddy look so pleased with himself.

"Maybe we could do it for ten minutes next time, instead of five?" Freddy said.

"Yeah," Renaldo agreed. "You just get started in five minutes and then the time is up."

"Ten or fifteen would be better than five," Audrey said, blushing. "Well, I got into it. I was finally writing fast, and I started seeing things that weren't in the painting. And you said we could fix these later, if we want, right?"

On Miss Lightstone's face was the slightest smile. "Yes, you'll have a chance to revise whatever you like."

"What about the fictional family trees?"

Antonio asked. "Are we still going to do those?"

Miss Lightstone glanced at the door while considering Antonio's question. She seemed less enthusiastic about this idea than she had been when it was first suggested.

"I'm not sure. Let me think about it. Mm?"

PANCAKES AND PORCUPINES

～

That night, as I was trying to fall asleep, I remembered that one of the first conversations I had with Antonio was in our backyard, when he was looking for evidence of something he had seen during the night: a white light in the sky that changed from round to thin, like a pancake.

So *that's* where that pancake had come from. I tried to remember what else he had described—there was something about giant red flowers—ah, yes, the flowers dripping yellow pollen.

It was unnerving to think that what he had seen was now so embedded in my brain that it felt, when I was writing in class, that I was seeing it, too, without any recollection that the scene had come from Antonio. It was also unnerving that we had chosen the same word (*deluge*) on the first day of writing experiments and the same image on this day and seen such similar scenes in our minds.

I tossed and turned. I couldn't sleep. Such a tangle of thoughts and images rolled around in my head.

The next morning, I was groggy. From the kitchen window, I saw a porcupine eating licorice—the red, whippy kind.

I poured cereal into two bowls and put them on the table.

Mom said, "Are you okay?"

"Yes."

"Are you sure?"

"Yes, absolutely." I poured us each a glass of juice.

"Do you mind if I don't eat the birdseed?"

"What?" I glanced at the contents of her bowl. "Oops."

"Maybe you should go back to bed, Gina."

"Yes, maybe I should."

I slept all day.

FICTIONAL TREES

～

One misty, foggy day, after we'd had tests in several other classes, Arif asked Miss Lightstone if we could finally do fictional family trees in her class. She seemed distracted and less energetic than usual, but asked Arif to put an example on the board, a template that others could follow.

At the board, he tapped his fingers against his legs for a minute. "This is just an example, right?" He didn't wait for anyone to answer but instead, in meticulous printing, he offered this suggestion:

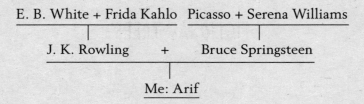

Arif turned and faced us, grinning. "Well, okay," he said, "you can see the problems there: people of different time periods and ages; names mixed up. Would J. K. Rowling have been J. K. White? Would Bruce Springsteen have been Bruce Picasso?"

"Wait," Margie said. "So in that example, are you saying that your mother is J. K. Rowling and your father is Bruce Springsteen?"

"Yeah."

"I've got one," Renaldo said, joining Arif at the board. "This one is with titles, not names."

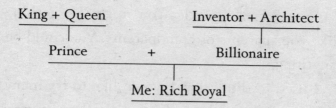

```
King + Queen              Inventor + Architect
       |                          |
    Prince        +          Billionaire
                  |
             Me: Rich Royal
```

Ruby elbowed Renaldo and Arif aside. "Maybe you don't turn out to be what your parents and grandparents are or were." She wrote:

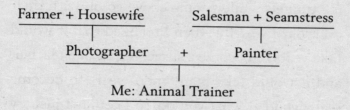

```
Farmer + Housewife        Salesman + Seamstress
        |                          |
  Photographer      +          Painter
                    |
             Me: Animal Trainer
```

Freddy raced to the board. "Okay, okay, then, what about this?"

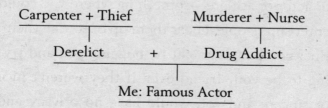

```
Carpenter + Thief         Murderer + Nurse
        |                        |
    Derelict        +       Drug Addict
                    |
             Me: Famous Actor
```

"See?" Freddy said. "You might be nothing like your parents or grandparents. You could be anything."

I used to think that I would like to try many different jobs, each one for six months or a year, like waitress and teacher and heart surgeon and cashier and even coal miner because what would that be like, being down inside the earth, making tunnels while people above go on with their everyday lives? But then I realized that it would take years to become a surgeon, say, or a teacher, and it would take many more years to become really good at what you do, so I couldn't just try on all these jobs for a few months at a time.

I used to think it would be fun to be a singer or actor or athlete—something where you could entertain people, cheer them up or soothe them. But then people might be bugging you and trying to be your friend even if they weren't nice or sincere and you would have no privacy and couldn't just go to the store when you wanted or get angry at someone in public and you might always be worrying if you were a good enough singer or actor or athlete.

And what if *What could you be?* didn't have anything at all to do with your job? What if it meant what kind of person you would be and what contributions you could or would make to the wider world around you?

I looked around the room. Why couldn't we all do noble things, important things? Why wouldn't we?

Why wouldn't I?

My own attempt at a fictional family tree resulted in many erasures because I could not decide what I might want to become.

Antonio also seemed frustrated. At last, he went to the board and drew a giant question mark.

"It was harder than I thought," he said.

For the rest of the class period, he remained silent and appeared preoccupied.

At lunch, I stood behind him in line. "Maybe," I said, "the less you know about your ancestors, the more free you would be to become anyone or anything."

He thought a minute. "But if you had too much choice—"

"Sometimes that is harder than too little choice. Isn't that what Miss Lightstone said?"

Who would he be?

Who could I be?

PREDICTIONS

~⌒~

A udrey, who was stick thin and white-pale and who had a soft heart and almost always wore light blue clothing, timidly approached Miss Lightstone one morning and said, "I didn't think redheads, like us, could wear that—that— orange color."

Miss Lightstone said, "Here is a secret: We redheads can wear any color we like. We can wear purple or black or aquamarine or carmine red or pink or yellow or any old color we like.

Isn't that brilliant?" She smoothed her orange polka-dotted skirt and her orange blouse.

Audrey nodded appreciatively, taking in this revelation.

"And," Miss Lightstone continued, quietly, "blondes can wear any color they like, and brunettes can and even gray-haired people can, too." She looked to the left and right as if she were revealing secrets and did not want to be overheard.

Audrey's mouth opened. Later, it closed.

Freddy asked if we could do fictional family trees again.

Miss Lightstone again looked left and right and whispered, "Yes. Not graded."

It felt grand, like a little mutiny.

At lunch, amid a clump of other students, Margie asked, "Well, what *would* I be or what *could* I be? I am having a hard time with that, even when I imagine that my grandfather was a king and my mother was an actress—"

Arif joined in. "Right. You wouldn't necessarily be *like* them at all."

Renaldo: "Or maybe, like if your father was a king, you would *have* to be a prince and later a king and you wouldn't have any choice, would you?"

Freddy: "Unless you defected. You could defect."

Margie repeated, mournfully, "What *could* I be?"

Antonio, who had been listening quietly, locked eyes with Margie and said, "You are very curious and you will make great discoveries about the moon."

In the quietest of voices, Margie said, *"Me?"*

"What about me, Antonio?" Arif asked. "What could I be?"

Antonio nodded, considering. "You will make great discoveries about our planet."

Freddy scoffed. "So is *everyone* going to make great discoveries, Antonio?"

"No," Antonio said. "You, for instance, will be celebrated for other reasons."

"Like being an actor? Like I wrote on the board?"

Others gathered round, curious about Antonio's "game," and a chorus of "Me? What about me? What could I be?" followed.

We learned that Ruby could—or would—work with animals and that Audrey (who had thus far not exhibited any musical ability) would be a singer. Renaldo would be a comedian or a teacher.

"A teacher?" Renaldo said. "Me?" He stood, hands on hips. "All right, everybody, listen up! Pay attention! We are never, ever having any more tests!"

More students gathered around asking, "Me?" Antonio studied each one briefly and then quietly but firmly announced his prediction.

Claire, who had been listening with a smirk on her face said, "So, everyone is going to be important. Everyone is going to be so—so—special." She glanced around at Antonio's audience. "Right," she added sarcastically.

"Not everyone," Antonio said, looking pointedly at Claire, who instantly deflated.

"That's mean," Claire said.

"Not intended to be mean—not everyone wants to be seen as important or special. Some people want to move along peacefully and quietly, without being slotted into any one mold."

Claire did not know what to make of this explanation. She stood up from the table and said, "If I want to be important or special, I will be."

At the end of the school day, as everyone was gathering books and jackets, Antonio stopped me.

"And you," he said, "why were you so quiet at lunch?"

"I was listening."

"Well, I'm glad you didn't ask me what you could or would be."

"And why not?" I expected him to feign horror, to tell me that my future could or would be too awful to contemplate.

He leaned toward me. He had the blackest eyes. He said, "Because *you* are a *mystery*."

"Good," I said.

KOMOREBI AND PASTA

꧁

September and its train of warm days and
nights had vanished, and into its place crept
the cooler days and cold nights of October. Trees
blazed orange and gold and red, and nearly every
day when the sun filtered through those leaves,
I stopped to acknowledge *komorebi*. I was not
alone in that. At the bus stop, inevitably someone would point out the light through nearby
trees and the dancing shadows on the ground.

"*Komorebi*—over there!"

"Komorebi!"

Soon the winds of November would arrive and send the leaves flying. Was there a word for that? Cascade? Deluge? Neither was quite right. The word needed to combine the cold, the wind, the whirling leaves.

At home, Dad kicked the furnace and shouted unmentionable words at it. We struggled to close stuck windows, accompanied by more unmentionable words from Dad.

"Do not listen," he said. "Do not use these words. These are words only for frustrated older people."

The weekly parade of pasta creations from the grandmother next door continued, despite my parents' attempts to stop them.

"Maybe you're not forceful enough," I suggested. "What did you say to her, Dad?"

"I said that her pasta was delicious, but that it was too much for us. She said, 'Nonsense! You can never have too much pasta.' She sounds just like Auntie Pasta."

"Maybe you need to say we are getting too fat."

"I tried that. She pinched my stomach and said, 'Well, only a little, but the *povera* Gina, she needs more fat on her!'"

We snuck portions out of the house to take to the Frails, but they no longer seemed so enchanted with our offerings.

"Oh, more—"

"Pasta."

"How very—"

"Very—"

"Um, generous—"

"And thoughtful—"

"But really there are others—"

"Yes, others who would benefit—"

"From your exceedingly generous—"

"And kind—"

"And delicious—"

"Offerings."

A day or two after our visits to the Frails, Miss Lightstone would again mention the "generosity and thoughtfulness" of Miss Judy, who had brought ravioli or cavatelli or lasagna to share with the faculty. When Antonio would turn immediately to me, I would erase from my face any indication of guilt.

I thought to myself, *shiyou ga nai*. It can't be helped, so why worry about it?

SMALL SECRETS

Antonio had been living next door for three months and although Dad had seen the grandmother on the weekly pasta deliveries, I had rarely seen her or Carlotta. Didn't they ever go out?

"Maybe they go out at night," Dad suggested. "Spies do that, you know."

"I thought spies liked to blend in with others, get people to trust them."

"Yes, there is that, too. They trick you into

137

letting your guard down and telling them your secrets. Maybe that is what the grandmother is doing by bringing us all that pasta. She is trying to make us spill the beans."

"On what?"

"I don't know. Maybe on how much money you are hiding in that little tin money box."

"Ha ha. Very funny."

"Most people have secrets, little ones mostly."

Was it a secret that sometimes, in the grocery store or the post office or even on the street, Dad would occasionally stop someone and say, "You dropped this." He would hand them five or ten dollars. We did not have a lot of money; this I knew from the unmentionable words he and Mom said to the monthly bills. But still, Dad saved some to carry in his pockets for the you-dropped-this routine.

Some people would say, "Oh, no, it isn't mine," and Dad would reply, "But I saw it fall from your pocket," and usually the person would look surprised and say, "Really? Huh. Well, thank you."

Some people quickly snatched the money and acted as if, of course, the money was theirs; how careless they were to drop it.

In time I learned that Dad was selective in his targets. Haggard-looking mothers trailing small, whining children were his favorites. Old men and women counting their pennies at the checkout seemed to "drop" ten-dollar bills frequently.

Was it a secret that Mom took flowers to the cemetery each Sunday morning and put them on two or three graves that had no flowers? I used to think she knew the people buried there, but when I asked her one day how she knew them, she said, "I don't know them, but somebody knew them. They were someone's son or daughter or sister or brother or mother or father, mm?"

MORE EXPERIMENTS

❧

One day a week in Miss Lightstone's class we did writing "experiments." I was increasingly eager for them, but Margie sometimes worried over them.

"I like to take my time," she said. "I like to figure out what I think before I write."

"But you can figure that out *while* you are writing fast," I said. "That's what I discovered, anyway."

"My mind doesn't work like that. My mind

doesn't like all that—that—messiness."

Miss Lightstone nodded sympathetically. "Messy mind is fine, Margie. Try it a few more times. You may find it easier, and maybe you'll find one gem in the middle of the mess, and later you can expand on that gem when you revise more slowly."

Our teacher wrote along with us and occasionally shared what she had written, like the day she chose "We didn't always live on Mango Street," but changed *Mango* to *Finchley.*

"Well, *that* was interesting," she said. "I wrote about the house I grew up in and I began remembering so many things, like the wallpaper in the kitchen was white with green ivy crawling up it, and once I drew little red-and-black ladybugs amid the leaves and it was a long time before anyone noticed those ladybugs and I loved having that little secret of the hidden ladybugs." Miss Lightstone put her hands on her heart. "I had completely forgotten those ladybugs."

Several people had chosen "In a hole in the ground there lived a hobbit" for their first line.

"The hobbit turned out to be evil—"

"My hobbit turned into a rabbit—"

"I wrote all about the hole and the tunnels and how a skunk wandered in one day."

Arif began with "There is no lake at Camp Green Lake," and perhaps because Antonio had recently predicted that Arif would make great discoveries about our planet, Arif wrote about terrifying changes in the ecosystem and about how all the lakes were gone and the oceans were shrinking and he needed to invent something that would reverse the process.

Fellow future discoverer Margie began with "Rendi was not sure how long the moon had been missing." She wrote about how long it took people to notice and what might have caused the moon to disappear and what she should do to investigate. How should she begin to look for a missing moon?

Ruby wrote about a missing horse, and when she held up her paper, you could see that she had written quick, short lines that looked like a poem:

Rendi was not sure
how long the horse
had been missing
missing horse
missing horse
who will miss
the horse
absent from the field
stuck stuck
stuckity stuck

Renaldo, potential future teacher, wrote, "My name is Prince Pablo SuperRendo but no one's ever called me that." It was important that no

one know his real name because he was working incognito as a teacher in an underprivileged
country, giving money to people anonymously.

That reminded me of my father and the
"dropped" money.

Freddy wrote, "We think they took my uncle."
He held up a page filled with words. "We think
he got deported," Freddy said. "For real."

We barely had time to sympathize when both
Audrey and Claire said they had chosen "I have
not had so good of a week,"[7] but they did not
want to discuss what they had written.

Antonio crumpled his paper and didn't want
to talk about what he had written either.

I wrote, "Their names are Marlene and Judy
but we call them the Frails." Pages of dialogue
spilled out of my brain. What they talked about
surprised me.

---

7. *Clementine*, Sara Pennypacker.

Miss Marlene:	Have you seen—
Miss Judy:	The surfboard?
Miss Marlene:	The good one.
Miss Judy:	I didn't take it.
Miss Marlene:	I didn't say you did.
Miss Judy:	I hated that surfboard.
Miss Marlene:	I hated your goat.

And then they started talking about the empress of Japan, but not in the nicest way:

Miss Marlene:	Did the empress of Japan ever—
Miss Judy:	Write a thank-you note?
Miss Marlene:	Did she?
Miss Judy:	I don't think so.
Miss Marlene:	A bit rude.
Miss Judy:	After all those cookies.

And somehow the writing then turned to the

two of them riding bicycles and going to the beach. They were so young.

At lunch, I asked Antonio what he had written about.

"The name one. You know, 'My name is—whatever—but no one ever calls me that.'"

"So why did you crumple it up?"

He reached into his pocket, pulled out the crumpled page, and handed it to me. It read, "I am a son, but no one ever calls me that."

I believe I responded with: "Oh! But—is that—are you—do you—?"

He didn't smile, but he leaned slightly toward me and said, in a soft voice, "It's okay. There are a lot of kids like me around."

THE CLACKERTYS

～

The next time Antonio's grandmother brought us a huge pan of lasagna, Dad said, "I know, I know, I should tell her to stop, but I can't do it, and we cannot eat anymore of it and we cannot burden the Frails with it again."

We looked sadly at the foil-covered pan, its contents enough to feed a dozen or more.

"Wait," Dad said. "I have an idea. We give it to a big family, a big hungry family, yes?"

"Like who?" I asked, but as soon as the

question came out of my mouth, I knew what
his answer would be.

"The Clackertys!" he said, triumphantly.
"There's a loud and crazy and big family for you.
Yes?"

"You're really going to walk down there and
hand them a pan of lasagna?"

"No, no, they don't want to see me invad-
ing with a big pan. I might scare them." A little
sheepish smile crept onto his face.

"Oh no," I said. "No, you don't. I won't. I
can't."

Dad gazed forlornly at the pan of lasagna.
He sighed a deep, heavy sigh and sat wearily
at the table. "Oh well," he said. "It was only
an idea. I was thinking of when I was little and my mother would make a big bowl of
cavatelli and meatballs and we would take it to
the neighbors who had a very big family, but
the husband had broken his arm and couldn't

work, and the momma always looked so tired. But you should have seen their faces when we showed up, me and my mother, with that big bowl of delicious-smelling pasta. You should have seen it, I tell you. They were hopping and laughing and so eager to taste that big bowl of delicious-smelling—"

"Okay, okay, okay," I said. "I'll take it to the Clackerty-Claffertys."

"Really? What a big, generous heart you have, Gina."

"Right."

Off I went, carrying the big pan of lasagna down the street, hoping Antonio's grandmother would not see me. I was still several houses away from the Clackertys when two of the little ones came charging at me, waving their muddy hands.

"Hi, hi, hi! Whatcha got? Whatcha got in that pan?"

"Is it snakes?"

"Is it turtles?"

I kept walking, weaving my way between them. Their yippy-yappy dog, trailing its leash, and two other Clackertys joined the young ones.

"Who's that? What's she got?"

"She has snakes and turtles!"

"And ribbity rabbits."

They were jumping up, trying to lift the edge of the foil, and the dog was jumping up, scratching my legs and tangling my feet in its leash.

Two other Clackertys jumped down from a tree. "Whatcha got there? Is that for us?"

"She's got snakes and turtles and ribbity rabbits and squishy snails."

At last I reached the porch and asked if their mother was home.

"Go on in," they said.

"She's probably on the couch. She's so tired!"

"Maybe you could put this in the kitchen," I suggested. "I don't want to bother her."

"She don't care! Everybody's always going in and out."

One of them opened the door and another pushed me forward. "Go on, couch is right over there."

"Mom, Mom, Mom, some girl is here—"

"With snakes and turtles—"

"No, no, I don't have snakes and turtles—"

A woman—Mrs. Clafferty, I assumed—was lying on the couch with a blanket over her legs. She did not get up, but she did open her eyes.

"We're not buying any," she said.

"No, no, I'm not selling—this is for you. It's lasagna."

Mrs. Clafferty sniffed the air. "Lasagna? Really?" She sat up. "For us? Why?"

One of the little kids said, "Aw, poo. No snakes? No turtles?"

"Where are the snakes and turtles and ribbity rabbits?"

Mrs. Clafferty said, "Thank you. Do you mind taking it to the kitchen? I broke my leg." She lifted the blanket to show me the cast. "Thank you so much."

"No snakes? No turtles?"

Two of the littles and the yippy-yappy dog followed me halfway back up the street.

"What's your name? Where do you live? Where are the snakes?"

At home, Dad said, "Success?"

"Next time, it's your turn."

CROWS

~&

Another package arrived from Nonna Filomena. In it was a delicate, narrow piece of
pale blue fabric, about a foot long, fringed with
tiny green and yellow beads. Dad translated
the attached note: "For your wrist, you wrap it
around. It is to ward off bad spirits."

I wrapped it around my wrist, instantly con-
vinced that it was infused with Nonna air and
angel air, with protection and strength.

In her accompanying letter, Nonna Filomena

related the latest Angel Lucia episode. Some of the villagers had been gossiping about a newcomer and the gossip grew and grew and became nastier and nastier.

Angel Lucia does not like this pettegolezzo—this gossip—so mean-spirited. She sends a hundred black crows to swarm the gossipers and to leave many splotches of—you know—the white slop—on their heads.

That angel, I loved her.

Also in the mail that day came a postcard from Auntie and Uncle Pasta, telling us that they were going to be passing through and would stay with us one night.

My parents were not amused. "No call to ask 'May we?' or 'Do you mind?'" Dad said. When Mom asked when they were arriving, Dad

154

examined the card. "Saturday. Nothing like a lot of notice. Saturday!"

Mom said, "Oh, rats. I do believe I have to work this weekend."

At school, my new wristlet was quickly noticed. Most people admired it and wanted to touch it, but a few, like Claire, were scornful.

"Another *special gift* from her nonna in Italy," Claire said. *"Tuh."*

Ruby said, "Even *I* could make *that—if* I wanted to."

Overhearing them, I stroked the material, confident that it would ward off their mean spirits.

Antonio asked if he could touch the cloth. He touched it lightly, gently, and the warmth of his touch went through the material to my wrist. He examined the beads. "Unusual," he said. "I like it."

Claire turned away. *"Tuh!"*

Ruby echoed her. *"Tuh!"*

Their spirit must have rubbed off on Freddy, for he said, "Look at that—Antonio wants a bracelet."

To my surprise, a few others chimed in, mocking Antonio, but Antonio ignored them.

My wrist was tingling.

There was a thump against the classroom window.

"A bird," someone said, "crashed into the—yikes—there are lots of them!"

A clump of crows flapping their shiny black wings and cawing, cawing darkened the window.

The next day, Margie and Audrey wore wristlets they had made from lavender cloth and sequins, and the following day more girls wore homemade wristlets. By the end of the week, even Claire and Ruby were wearing them.

Antonio wore his own version: a white wristband—the kind that tennis players wore—dotted with blue and black circles.

UNCLE AND AUNTIE PASTA RETURN

❧

Dad and I had barely finished cleaning the house when Uncle and Auntie Pasta arrived. Mom was conveniently at work.

In they charged with a rush of groans and chatter and jostling: *Oof*, her coat was too hot; *Ack*, Uncle bumped his elbow; *Bah*, the traffic was terrible; *Oof*, her throat was so dry; *Unh*, she needed her medicine . . .

They brought, as usual, two gifts for me: lacy, white socks and another quarter for the tin bank. Auntie demanded that I try on the socks and remarked that my feet had grown *so large*. If my feet weren't *so large* the socks would fit better.

Uncle demanded to see the tin money box, which he handled as if it contained precious gems. He shook it. "Seems like there should be more in there. Have you taken any out? I hope you have not. You must save, save, save! Go on, put in the new deposit." He watched as I inserted the quarter into the slot. "Good, good, now don't take that out."

Uncle said he was so hungry he could eat a moose, and Auntie said that moose would taste terrible, and he asked her how she knew that, and she said, "I just know it." In response to his dire hunger, Auntie unpacked the flour and eggs and tomatoes and basil and olive oil. She rolled up her sleeves.

"Okay!" she said. "Now I make—guess!"

Dad and I exchanged weary looks. He said, "Hm, let me think—I know! You're going to make roast beef."

"*Pah!* I am not making roast of beef."

Picking up Dad's game, I said, "Fried chicken?"

"*Pah!*"

In turn, we guessed beef stew, chicken noodle soup, and chocolate cake, and each time she said, "*Pah!*"

Uncle Pasta was perched on a rickety chair in the corner of the kitchen, rubbing his foot and looking at us as if we had lost our minds.

Finally, Uncle said, "*Pah, pah, pah!* Don't be imbeciles. She is making *pasta*!"

"Ohhh," Dad said, "pasta," and with less enthusiasm, I echoed him. "Oh, pasta."

"I know you have been hoping for my pasta," Auntie said. "I make it for you, even though my back is hurting and my hands are swollen and my head is pounding. Do you have some aspirin?"

During dinner they talked nonstop. We heard about Auntie's cousin Guadalupe with the big nose, and about the neighbor who had been shot outside her apartment (she moved and a nasty lady moved in) and about the people they were going to visit in Indiana (very fine people from Sweden).

Auntie said that she and Uncle were feeling invisible.

"Invisible?" Dad said. "What do you mean?"

Auntie patted her face and her hair. "Look at our wrinkles and our gray hair. We are not *so* old, you know, but people see the wrinkles and the gray hair and they either think, 'Oh, they are old and worthless now, what can they do?' or they don't see us at all. Isn't that right?" She poked her fork at Uncle. "Tell them."

161

Uncle nodded. "Invisible," he said. "Worth-less." He contemplated his plate.

I felt sorry for things I had thought.

"You're not worthless or invisible," I said.

Auntie dabbed at her eyes with her napkin and passed two meatballs to my plate.

HOBBIT HOLES

~

The next time we wrote in class I chose the sentence about the hobbit hole and changed it a bit:

In a hole in the ground there lived the Hobbit family: Mr. and Mrs. Hobbit and their seven children. Everywhere they went, they all went together, a chain of Hobbits winding through the woods and through the town, and often they had to stop and wait for one or two or three stragglers who were chasing ribbity rabbits and snakes and stuck stuck stuck stuck—

Wait! I think I did this when I was young. I think I had an imaginary family of—not hobbits, but tiny people, barely six inches tall. And I think they had names, yes, there was Mrs. Tannerobby and her many children—I forget how many—but they had names—there was, let me think think think think—oh, there was Clove and Stick and who was that messy one, was it Unicorn Marie or something like that? And there was Herfy and and and . . .

Whenever we would go anywhere, the Tannerobbys had to come along and sometimes we had to wait to find one or another and sometimes they would argue . . . and sometimes Mom would say, "Can't the Tannerobbys stay home today?" and I would say, "Oh, no, they would be too lonely."

∽

When writing time was up, I was not the only dazed one who had to blink myself back to the world of the classroom. People were talking all at once:

"*Komorebi* and lightning and *mångata* trails—"

"The street that we didn't always live on was Broken Tree Road and a horrible thing happened there—"

"I remembered the house my grandmother lived in—"

"There was no lake at Camp Green Lake, but there was a swamp that swallowed people."

At lunch Antonio said, "Hobbit hole?"

"Yes. You?"

"Of course." He tapped his head and pointed at mine, as if to say, *Our brains are connected*.

SILENCE

~

Occasionally Miss Lightstone would close her eyes and press two fingers to the center of her forehead. "Sometimes there is too much noise in the world, don't you think?" she once said.

Another time she said, "Did you ever notice how *much* people *talk?* Does it all start to sound like—like—buzzing?"

Margie said, "Yes, you're right! All the time, people talk, talk, talk. Some people never shut up."

All heads swiveled toward Freddy.

"I do *not* talk all the time. What about Ruby? There's a real chatterbox for you!"

Heads swiveled to Ruby.

"*Me*? Are you *kidding*? What about—?"

Miss Lightstone wisely interrupted. "How about we try an experiment? I'm not sure it's possible, but what if we all—each one of us— tried to be quiet for a whole hour? Do you think we could do it?"

"That's *easy*!" Freddy said. "So easy it's ridiculous. How about two hours? Or three? Or a whole day?"

That is how we came to an agreement that each Wednesday at school would be Silent Day in Miss Lightstone's class. It was not as easy as it might sound.

If we had questions, we couldn't just write them down and take them up to Miss Lightstone for her to answer. We had been trooping back and forth, back and forth, until Miss Lightstone closed her eyes, stabbed two fingers into her forehead, and then wrote on the board:

A written question is also noise. Try to answer your own questions today.

The next day, Ruby felt obliged to report that her father did not think it appropriate for a teacher to refuse to answer questions.

Miss Lightstone assured us that she would be happy to answer questions on all the other days of the week, and that it might be "an interesting experiment" to see if we could answer our own questions instead of blurting them out whenever they popped into our heads.

"I don't *blurt*," Ruby said.

"I was not referring to you, personally, Ruby."

Each Wednesday, on the board, was a list of things we were to do in class. For example, we could read, do a writing experiment, or revise something we'd previously written.

We fidgeted through that first Wednesday, trying to adjust to this new arrangement. I hadn't thought it would be difficult to remain quiet. I relished the thought that some of the chatterers would have to be silent.

After a few blissful silent minutes, I heard tapping:

Foot tapping.

Pencil tapping.

Finger tapping.

I heard:

Yawning.

Coughing.

Throat clearing.

I heard the *tick-tick-tick* of the clock at the front of the room.

I heard my own breathing.

I heard other people's breathing.

The silence was so *noisy*.

ABSENCE

~

Antonio was not at the bus stop one morning and he was not at school all day. People kept asking me where he was, as if I was his keeper. In frustration, I finally said, "How would *I* know?" to which Claire replied, "Don't you live next door to him?"

Audrey chimed in, "I thought you *loved* him!"

"I do *not* love him."

"Do you know if he will be here later?"

"No. I have no idea."

At lunch, Ruby asked, "Where's Antonio? Is he sick?"

Standing in line behind me, Freddy said, "I wish someone would notice when *I* was absent. Nobody notices if I don't show up."

"Sure, they do, Freddy," I said.

"No, they don't."

And the sad thing was, he might have been right.

When I got home that day, a girl with orange hair and a bright yellow raincoat was standing in Antonio's backyard spraying Mr. Blue, the cat, with a hose. The cat dashed this way and that, either dodging the spray or trying to drink from it. It was hard to tell which.

"Hi," I said. "Where's Carlotta?"

The girl turned to me, tilted her head from one side to the other. "Carlotta? Where is she? Well, she just up and flew away"—she waved her hand in the air —"just like that. Like a bird. Or a fly. Or whatever."

I stepped closer. "Are you—?"

She put up her hand like a stop sign. "Whoa. Close enough."

"It *is* you," I said. "Carlotta? I didn't recognize you, what with—with—you know, the new hair and all."

She pulled a chunk of hair to one side. "This is *new*?"

"I mean the color—the color is new, right?"

"Whatever," she said.

"Is Antonio home? Is he sick?"

She squinted at me and swished the hose so that the water landed near my feet. "Antonio who?"

At night I dreamed that I was writing my life. I would be writing rapidly—long, detailed passages about places and people. I wasn't writing about things that had happened, but about what was *about to happen*. As soon as I wrote something, it appeared before me.

If I described a tiger, it appeared: sleek and mysterious and elegant. If I described a person named, say, Georgio, he would appear in our class or at my house.

In my dreams, I realized that I could *create* my life in this way. Anything could happen, good or bad. Anyone could appear, for good or ill.

When I woke, the feeling of that mystery, of that ability to create my life, lingered. It was an odd feeling, as if something were growing inside me—in my mind or my body or my soul—or all of those. I liked the feeling but I also feared it.

Antonio was not at school the next day or the next.

In Miss Lightstone's class, we now wrote for thirty or forty minutes and still, for many of us, that wasn't enough time, and we were frustrated when the time was up.

"I was just getting to something interesting."

"I have to finish this."

Miss Lightstone, who wore a ladybug pin on writing days, said, "The ladybug inspires me—ever since that time we were writing and I remembered the wallpaper on which I drew ladybugs."

Freddy wrote with increasing intensity, sometimes exclaiming aloud "Whoa!" or "Wow!"

"I feel like I'm *on fire*," Arif said one day. "Like I could just write and write and write and even if some of it later sounds stupid, so what? In the middle are some cool things."

"Surprising things," Margie agreed. "Like all of a sudden the old lady who lives next door popped up when I was writing about our street. I described what she looked like, what she wore, how she sat on the porch in a metal chair, how she talked, that funny accent . . ."

And I understood, because that was happening to me, too.

But Antonio was not there, and I missed him.

RIBBITY RABBITS

On Saturday, three of the younger Clackerty children appeared at our door: two boys and a girl (or it might have been three boys or three girls; it was hard to tell).

"Is the girl home?" they asked Mom. "The one with the ribbity rabbits and the snakes?"

"Uh, I'm not sure who—"

"And the lasagna?"

"Oh, I think you mean Gina. Is that who you mean?"

"Is she the one with the ribbity rabbits and snakes and turtles?"

I joined Mom at the door.

"There she is! That's her! Do you have some ribbity rabbits and snakes and turtles?"

"Not today," I said.

"Lasagna? Do you have lasagna today?"

"Ah. Try next door. Ask for the grandmother. She makes the best lasagna."

A short time later, the three Clackertys returned.

"The grandma is not there. Only a girl with orange hair."

"Like a pumpkin."

"Pumpkin hair."

"And a mean cat."

"Really, really mean. See?" A boy revealed scratches on his arm. "I was just trying to hold it."

"And the cat went crazy—"

177

"And the pumpkin hair girl—"
"Was snotty—"
"Snotty snot snot-head—"
"And she didn't have any lasagna—"
"And even if she did—"
"She wouldn't give it to us—"
"Snotty snot-head."

THE HOLE IN THE ROOM

❦

School was different without Antonio.

When someone asked a question or made a comment in Miss Lightstone's class, we often turned automatically toward Antonio's desk.

When had that become a habit, to look to Antonio for affirmation? Were we seeking confirmation that he heard us?

Were we seeking his approval?

Why did he matter so much to us?

Why did I feel sad or betrayed by his absence?

There was a hole in the room where he had been.

One day, Renaldo sat at Antonio's desk.

"Hey!" Freddy said. "You can't do that."

"Why not?"

"Because that's—that's Antonio's place."

"So?"

Arif said, "It doesn't seem right."

Others had gathered near, murmuring disapproval.

"You shouldn't sit there."

"He might come back today."

"No," Miss Lightstone said, entering the room. "Not today. Maybe next week. There is some sort of family business to attend to."

"Someone died, I bet," Arif said.

November was cold and gray. In Miss Lightstone's class, we wrote and wrote. One time she said, "Basketball players practice dribbling, yes? Today let's dribble with words."

Another time: "Tennis players practice strokes: forehand, backhand, volley, serve. Over and over. Let's practice our sentence strokes."

Sometimes she met with us individually while the others were working. She would say, "What a strong detail" or "Which part do you like the best?" or "This sounds like a poem" or "I'd love to know more about this place" or "I hope you will write more about that."

One time she said to me, "You notice things. You wonder about people. You are a good observer."

When she moved on to the next person, I stared down at my notebook, repeating her words in my head. Instinctively, I turned to Antonio's seat, wanting to share that moment with him, hoping he had heard her.

But Antonio was not there.

Sometimes we worked in pairs or small groups, listening to each other's work, seeking something special in each piece. I was often surprised by what I heard.

I liked the way Renaldo wrote dialogue, his pieces like short plays. Freddy's pieces, I thought, would be sarcastic, and at first they were, but something gradually changed so that by the end of that month, he was writing a mystery, filled with eerie landscapes and hidden clues. Its first sentence was, "In a hole in the ground lay the wooden chest."

Margie and Arif both wrote detailed, specific descriptions of places they had lived and people they had known. I could see these places and these people, and I could hear Margie's and Arif's voices in them, too.

When I was writing, I could follow the rhythms of my own mind, and I could explore people and worlds with abandon. I could be funny or silly or serious. I could be anyone or anything.

Miss Lightstone strolled by our desks and stopped to say, "Oh, why don't you read that line there, Arif? I like that detail." Or "Margie, what was that beautiful line you wrote about the blue scarf on the white-haired lady?"

Now when Miss Lightstone would ask, "Who has a contribution they would like to offer?" most of us had something to volunteer. It felt so worthy to have a *contribution*.

Those days in her class seemed to balance the flatness of November skies.

But Antonio was still gone.

ANYONE HOME?

~

Each day I looked for signs of life at Antonio's house. Occasionally, I'd notice a curtain had been opened or closed, but no people emerged, and even Mr. Blue, the cat, was nowhere around. Leaves littered the yard where they had fallen weeks earlier.

One day I saw the mailman delivering mail there. When he came to our house, I said, "I'm not sure anyone still lives there—next door."

"Oh?" He turned to regard the house. "Well,

they're still getting mail. We don't have a change-of-address notice for them, and until we do, I guess we'll still deliver there."

I studied his face, taking note of thick eyebrows and wide nose. I wondered how I would describe him in writing.

"No packages for you today, Miss Gina Filomena," he announced with a flourish. "But I do have a few bills. I am hoping you are not the one who has to pay them."

The following day I marched up to Antonio's front door and knocked loudly. I was tired of waiting and wondering. I knocked again and again, louder each time. I sat on the front steps and waited. When I thought I heard a noise inside, I knocked again.

The door opened slightly.

"*What?* What do you *want?*"

It was Carlotta, her hair no longer orange but now jet black and cut in jagged angles, as if someone had hacked at it with a dull knife. She squinted at me, her face distorted with annoyance.

"Why are you endlessly *knocking*? Is there an emergency? Is this house burning down? What do you *want*?"

"I need to know about Antonio."

"You *need* to? Why on earth would you *need* to?"

"At school—we were wondering—when he would be returning."

"Is that so? At school people were *wondering*. Not you, specifically?"

"Are you okay?" I asked.

"Oh, for heaven's sake," she spluttered. "I have no idea when he'll be back or *if* he'll be back." And with that, she shut the door and I heard the lock click.

WOOZY

~⁓

I had the flu. For five days, I slept and woke
and wobbled and slid in and out of fever and
chills and confusion and fog. I was dimly aware
of Mom's and Dad's presence and their soothing
voices and their faces with their troubled brows
bent close to mine.

Full moons and lighted paths of reflection on
dark lakes filled my dreams. In this woozy state,
I met Angel Lucia and an elephant with a frog
on its head and a porcupine eating red licorice.

Glimpsing a group of students at the bus stop, I called to them: "Wait, wait for me—" but they did not hear me and the bus came and went without me. "Wait—" I called. "Wait! I have a *contribution*!"

MISSED

~❦~

When I returned to school, I learned that both
Margie and Arif had come to my house to
check on me while I was absent, but no one had
answered the door.

"It was spooky," Margie said, "as if you'd dis-
appeared."

"But Miss Lightstone told us you were sick,"
Arif added.

And then I caught sight of Antonio's desk and
inhaled so suddenly and deeply that I choked.

"He's—he's back?" I said.

"Who?" Arif said.

Margie leaned against me. "That's the new boy. His name is Gerald."

Arif whispered, "He's not very friendly."

I had to see for myself.

On top of a long, lanky body was a tangle of dusty brown hair, like a dirty mop. He had squinty eyes and a beak nose and hollowed cheeks. When I approached, his head jerked up.

"What?" he said. "Whaddya want?"

His voice was hoarse, as if he'd been shouting.

"I'm Gina. I've been sick. You're new?"

"Well, I'm not *old*," he snarled.

"I meant new to this school—"

"I knew what you meant."

"Your name is . . . ?"

"Gerald."

"Do people call you Jerry?"

"No. They call me Gerald."

He didn't deserve that desk.

I felt I had missed much more than a week of school because I did not understand the references others were making to a book they had read or to pieces they had written.

Apparently Arif had developed a complex fictional world of castles and knights and treachery. When he offered to read a passage on the day I returned, I was confused.

"Wait—who are the good knights?"

"Oh, you missed all that, Gina. You'd have to read the whole thing from the beginning."

Margie was writing a story about an old woman with magical powers.

"Wait—can she actually transform people into animals?"

"Oh, you missed all that, Gina. I'll fill you in later."

Others were especially interested in Freddy's story about the hidden chest in a hole in the ground.

"Wait, are the badgers good or bad?"

"Oh, you missed all that, Gina."

"His story is really good, and you missed all that, Gina."

The new boy, Gerald, was cranky when it came to writing time.

"I hate to write."

And:

"Writing is a bore."

And:

"I don't get what the words and pictures on the board are supposed to do."

Miss Lightstone met separately with him to explain, but he resisted her help.

"It just seems so stupid," he said, pinching his beaky nose, as if offended by a smell.

"Ah," Miss Lightstone said. "Freddy? Tell Gerald how you used to feel about our experiments."

Freddy was engrossed in writing his story. "What? Oh. Yeah, I used to think it was stupid, too." He bent his head toward his paper. "But it isn't."

Gerald crossed his arms. "My hand hurts."

"Let's try writing fast for one minute. Do you think you could manage one minute?" Miss Lightstone asked.

"Doubt it."

Snotty snot-head.

On that first day back, I was out of practice and unable to concentrate. From the board, I chose the words *reflection* and *illusion* and stumbled around getting stuck stuck stuck and then started writing about being sick and about how the world around me seemed hazy then, and about Antonio and his distinct smile and the way it slowly, steadily revealed itself, as if it was triggered by the person he was talking with.

And that seemed profound to me, that realization that something in him was responding to something he saw in the other person, and in turn, it allowed that person to see something in him.

I glanced over at the new boy, Gerald, scowling, stiff and stubborn. Was his expression a reflection of him or of how he felt about the people around him? Or both?

At the end of the day, I realized that not a single person had mentioned Antonio.

DELIVERY BOY

~ى

At home, flour and eggs and onions and garlic and ground beef and tomatoes littered the countertops.

"Are Uncle and Auntie Pasta here?" I probably sounded alarmed. My mind was already racing through the mess in my room, the sheets that needed washing, and our general unpreparedness for such a visit.

"No, no, Gina, don't worry. No visitors."

"Then—what is all this?"

Dad looked a little sheepish. "Since we are not getting any batches of pasta from next door, I was getting hungry for some. Yes, it is true. Don't look at me like that. I couldn't help it." With a flourish, he offered me a plate of cinnamon toast and a cup of cocoa. "See? I did not forget the need for toast and cocoa."

The toast and cocoa were comforting, as was the routine, and afterward we made the pasta and sauce. Dad wanted to know how my first day back at school was, and so I told him about the fuzziness of it and about the new boy, Gerald, and very quietly at the end, I added that no one had spoken of Antonio.

"As if he never existed, Dad."

"Ah."

"I don't see how that can be. He made such a—a—such a *contribution* to—"

"To what? To your school? Your class?"

"To—"

"What, Gina? To your world?"

I could only nod and sniffle and wipe my eyes.

"You are getting sauce on your face," Dad said.

We made too much pasta and too much sauce.

"Who do we give the rest to?" Dad wondered.

"Your turn to take it to the Clackertys," I said.

"Okay, okay."

"And maybe Carlotta next door? She probably hasn't had any pasta lately either."

"You do that one," Dad said.

I remembered my last encounter with Carlotta. "Maybe you could do both?"

He dabbed at my cheek with a towel. "Okay, okay. I will be Mr. Delivery Boy."

When Dad returned from his pasta delivery to the Clackertys, he quickly locked the door. His hair was sticking up, his shirt untucked and pasta stained, his shoes untied.

"Quick," he said. "Hide! We're not home!" Closing the curtains in the front room, he raced to the back door and locked it as well.

"What is it?"

He bent, hands to knees, to catch his breath.

Knocks on the front door.

"No, don't get it, Gina! Quick! Upstairs! Hide!"

I followed him upstairs.

"Tell me! What is it? Who is it? What is happening?"

"Shh. Wait. Listen."

Knocks on the back door. I crept to the hall window, which overlooked that door.

"Dad, it's only the Clackertys—the little ones."

"*Only?* Shh. They'll hear you."

From below came shouts from the littles.

"Pasta man! Pasta man!"

"Come out, come out!"

"Pasta man!"

Dad slumped against the wall and slid to the floor, where he sat, a dazed lump of a man. He whispered, "Those kids will eat you alive! They are very hungry!"

After Dad had recovered from his visit to the Clackertys, and after he had checked that none of them were lurking outside our house, he took another batch of pasta to Carlotta next door. Barely five minutes later, he returned home, the pasta pan still in his hands.

"Gina, this is a strange day."

"Carlotta didn't want the pasta? That seems awfully rude."

"It wasn't Carlotta."

"Was it a girl? Did she have black hair all crazy-chopped?"

"It was a girl. *Blue* hair. Crazy-chopped."

"That's Carlotta," I said.

"She said Carlotta did not live there."

"Did she say what her name was?"

"Princess Azalea."

"Ha!"

"No, really, Gina, that is what she said her name was and she seemed quite serious."

"And the pasta?"

"She hates pasta. She was very polite about it, though. She said, 'Sir, I am sorry to disappoint, but I, Princess Azalea, have a strong dislike of— of—*pasta*.' She said *pasta* as if the word itself tasted bad."

SUKEY

~o

At school the next day I chose the word *reflection* and began writing about Carlotta and Princess Azalea and how maybe one was a reflection of the other. Maybe Princess Azalea was Carlotta's better self. Soon, however, a bucket of unexpected thoughts from kindergarten poured out.

On the first day of kindergarten, when I came home from school, Mom asked me how the day had been. I replied that it was okay. "Most kids were good."

"*Most* kids?"

"Yes, except for Sukey."

"What did Sukey do?"

"She didn't pay attention. Miss Lockett had to keep saying, 'Sukey! Are you paying attention? You need to pay attention to this.'"

"She'll get used to it," Mom said. "It can be hard at first."

"And Sukey kept dropping things, like her pencil and her crayons and her paper, and when Miss Lockett reminded her to pick them up, Sukey said she was too tired."

For the next few weeks, I eagerly gave my parents daily updates on Sukey's behavior.

"Sukey fell asleep, right in the middle of story time! Miss Lockett said, 'Wake up, wake up, sleepyhead.' Everyone laughed except for Sukey, who was very, very sleepy."

Another day: "Sukey scribbled on her desk, and Miss Lockett told her that she would need to wash that off, and from then on, she should only scribble on paper. Sukey said she wasn't scribbling, she was drawing."

Another day: "Sukey punched a boy, but she said the boy had punched her first, and the boy said he hadn't, and Miss Lockett said that punching was not permitted in our classroom. Not ever."

A few weeks later, Mom went to Parents' Night at the school and saw Miss Lockett. When Mom came home, she said, "Strangest thing— when I mentioned that I'd heard all about Sukey, she said, 'Sukey? Who is that?'"

"Hm."

"She did remember you, though," Mom said. "She said you had a wonderful imagination but that you seemed tired sometimes and had a little trouble settling in to all the rules of the class-room, but that you were adjusting."

"Hm. She said all that?"

"Yes."

"Hm."

Afterward, when Mom or Dad would ask about my day, I'd say it had been fine, and that I had used my imagination a lot.

"And Sukey?" they would ask.

"She's adjusting," I said.

All of that emerged from bouncing off one word: *reflection*. It seemed magical, the way a word could open up paths in my mind and lead to places and people both old and new.

I felt as if the tiny tin box of my mind was breeding riches.

ADJUSTING

～⌒

Next I wrote about *adjusting*, leaping off my recollection of Sukey and of adjusting to kindergarten and how maybe we were always adjusting: to new teachers and students and classes, to everyone we encountered, to noises, to weather, to food.

I wondered what or who shaped us or were we shaping ourselves?

I thought about Antonio and how I no longer expected to see him at the bus stop or at his desk.

I thought about how no one spoke of him, as if they were angry with him for having deserted us with no warning or explanation.

"Gina?" Miss Lightstone knelt beside my desk. "You okay?"

She handed me a tissue and patted my arm.

"I'm just adjusting."

"To—?"

"Life."

Miss Lightstone patted my arm again. "Ah, life," she whispered. "Yes, one is always adjusting."

Always?

At the end of each day, Miss Lightstone still traced beneath the two lines that had been up there on the board for so long now:

Who are you?
Who could you be?

Had we so *adjusted* to those lines that we no longer were conscious of them? I was absently staring at the lines when I realized the question on the board wasn't "Who am *I*?" but "Who are *you*?"

Confused, I looked all around the room. I didn't want to write about myself or what I knew anymore. I wanted to write about who and what I did *not* know.

On the bus on the way home that day, I asked Margie a question that had been nagging at me.

"Why doesn't anyone mention Antonio?"

Margie said, "Oh, Gina."

Arif, sitting in front of us, turned around and said, "You must have missed all that."

"All what?"

Margie said, "It must have been while you were sick."

Arif explained that many of them had been

moaning and groaning about missing Antonio, and one day a fight broke out when Freddy said he did not see what the big deal was with Antonio.

"And Audrey punched Freddy, and Freddy punched Renaldo, and someone threw Freddy's books on the floor—"

"And I was trying to defend Freddy," Margie said, "but then he said Antonio was *weird*, and someone else agreed—"

"And everyone was yelling."

And that was when Miss Lightstone suggested they all settle down and spend the next half hour writing about what was bothering them.

Margie was clutching my arm as if I might float out the window. "I think most of us ended up writing about Antonio, but no one wanted to share what they had written."

"I wrote about the way he listened to people and about the cool things that came out of his head," Arif said.

"And I wrote about that smile—the slow, widening one. You know what I mean?"

I knew.

"But at lunch, Claire said she had written about how strange Antonio seemed to her, and someone else said that Antonio claimed he saw weird things—like elephants and porcupines."

"And even though I didn't mean to," Arif admitted, "I mentioned the time Antonio said he felt the world turning."

"After all that, we stopped talking about Antonio, I guess," Margie said. "But that was when you were sick, Gina, so you missed all that."

THE KNIGHT, THE LION,
AND THE BADGER

Over the course of the next week, as students volunteered to read from the stories they were writing, I began to see a pattern.

In Arif's story of a castle threatened by an evil army was a magnificent hero: the Knight of Onio. He was strong and powerful, but also quiet and noble. When he smiled at people—friend or foe—they acquired some of his strength.

Margie wrote of an old, old woman whose touch could transform people into creatures that mirrored their personalities: a pacing tiger, a shy lamb, a sneaky fox. The only person not affected by her touch was a young man who had appeared on her doorstep one morning, offering to chop wood. The young man had a magnetic smile that cast its own spell on the old woman, transforming her into . . . something. Margie was not yet sure what that would be.

Freddy's story of the chest hidden in the ground told of the Badgers—a band of lost boys who were the rightful heirs to the chest. Their leader was a boy named Santon, who was really a traitor in disguise. He was tall and lean with black curly hair that draped over one eye.

So.

They had not forgotten Antonio. He had become a character in their stories. I wondered what other parts of their lives were in their stories.

Meanwhile, the new boy, Gerald, who hated

writing, now drew while the rest of us wrote. At first, he wouldn't show anyone his drawings, but as the days went on, we glimpsed portions of his work. He drew faces reflected in mirrors and sun-ray daggers piercing leaves and winding mazes through forests. When he drew intricate tunnels into the earth, leading to an underground dwelling, something clicked. I said, "You're using the inspiration boards, right?"

Arif walked over to Gerald's desk and read, "In a hole in the ground lived—"

"But it's not a hobbit," Gerald said, covering his paper with one arm. "I'm definitely *not* going to have any stupid *smiling* people in here, though."

Snotty snot-head.

But . . .

His drawings *were* very good.

THE TRIAL SMILE

As I fell asleep that night, I thought about Antonio's smile and how it had affected so many, and it occurred to me that I could try an experiment. Why couldn't *I* smile like that?

The next morning, Mom said, "What are *you* so happy about?"

"Oh, nothing."

"Why are you smiling so much?"

"Can't a person smile for no reason?"

At the bus stop, Margie said, "What are *you*

so happy about? It's freezing out here."

At school, Freddy said, "What? What are *you* looking at? What are *you* smiling about?"

Even Miss Lightstone said, "Gina, have you had some good news?"

Everyone turned to look at me.

I removed the smile.

At lunch, Renaldo whispered to me, "I know what you're doing—with the smiling. You're imitating Antonio, aren't you?"

"It's an experiment. Want to join me?"

After lunch:

Freddy: "What's so funny, Renaldo?"

Arif: "Yeah, why the big smile? Did you play a joke on somebody?"

Claire: "What are you up to, Renaldo?"

Margie: "Do you and Gina have some secret you're not telling us?"

Neither Margie nor Arif spoke to me the rest of the day.

Renaldo and I stopped smiling.

The next day at the bus stop, Margie and Arif were smiling.

"What are *you* so happy about?" I asked.

Margie and Arif replied in unison, "Nothing. Nothing."

At school, Ruby asked them what was so funny. "What's the big joke?"

Claire: "Is this some stupid game? Cut it out."

They removed their smiles.

On the following day, it was Ruby and Audrey, smiling all over the place.

"Hi!" Ruby said. Smile.

"Hey there!" Audrey crooned. Smile.

Arif said, "Not funny. Cut it out."

They removed their smiles.

That day Gerald drew a ten-panel cartoon that

showed various people grinning and smiling, their mouths stretched ridiculously wide. Along came a tall, armored figure, brandishing a sparkling sword.

"Enough!" the armored figure boomed. "Off with the smiles!" The figure waved his sword in the air, flipping and twirling it, and as the sword spun past each person, the smiles vanished.

The final cartoon panel was blank. Gerald had not decided how to finish it.

"Hmm," Miss Lightstone murmured. "Hmm."

Quickly Gerald sketched the final panel. It showed a row of expressionless people with blank stares.

"Huh," Gerald said. "I wasn't quite expecting that result. Looks like a bunch of sheep."

"Gray and dirty?" I asked.

"What?"

"Oh, nothing."

THE DESK

~∘

An extra desk appeared in our classroom overnight.

"What's with that?" Freddy asked.

Miss Lightstone looked up from her attendance book, squinted at that empty desk, and said, "Hmm."

At the classroom door, Miss Judy appeared, and with a wave of her slender fingers, summoned Miss Lightstone to the hall. When our teacher returned, Renaldo asked her if she was in trouble.

"Trouble? *Moi?*" She absently touched the ladybug pin on her collar. "No trouble. No trouble whatsoever."

"And the extra desk? What's with that?"

"Oh, we might have an extra student tomorrow, that's all."

"Extra student?"

"Who is it?"

"Boy or girl?"

"Is it temporary? Like for one day only?"

Miss Lightstone said, "Let's write, mm?"

We wrote.

I was on a dark path, closed in on all sides by thick trees, when suddenly the moon broke through with a bright shaft of light, illuminating a stranger on the path.

At lunch, it became clear that a stranger had entered several other stories that day:

In Arif's castle story, the stranger was the long-lost father of the Knight of Onio.

In Margie's story of the old woman, the young man with the magnetic smile turned her into a complete stranger, someone she did not recognize.

In Freddy's story of the hidden chest in the hole in the ground a ghostly figure appeared. He called himself the Extra.

Later, at the bus stop, Arif said, "I hope the extra student is friendlier than Gerald."

ONE TIME

❦

The next morning the extra desk remained unoccupied.

"Ohhh," Margie moaned. "Where is the extra? I was hoping for some excitement this morning."

Audrey and Ruby lingered by the empty desk. "Do you think it'll be a boy or a girl?"

Gerald brushed past them, plonking books onto his own desk.

"Poor kid," he said.

I was restless, eager to write that morning,

eager to calm my jumbled thoughts. How did a person make sense of things?

One time, when some were having trouble getting started with writing practice, Miss Lightstone said, "You might want to try what Gina does."

Heads swiveled to stare at me. I wanted to evaporate.

Miss Lightstone continued, "Try starting with 'One time': One time I did this . . . or saw that or . . . whatever. Just concentrate on that one time."

I did that?

Arif and Margie and Renaldo looked genuinely intrigued. Claire and Ruby did not. They zinged jagged eyebrow beams at me.

Later, when I leafed through my notebook, I saw that Miss Lightstone was right. I did often begin with "One time . . ."

Maybe I could shape my jumbled life into a

string of *one time*s. All the separate pieces—like Miss Lightstone and Antonio and Margie and Arif and Miss Judy and Auntie Pasta and the Clackertys and Angel Lucia and Nonna Filomena and the elephants and porcupines and *mångatas* and Sukeys and Tannerobbys and lasagna and ribbity rabbits and all of it—what did they all add up to? Could they loop and connect and make sense of me?

I was trying to catch up with my brain, trying to make my way through the tangles, when one word popped into my head and flashed there like a neon sign: *writer*.

And as I sat back to marvel at that one word, Miss Judy appeared at the door, waving to Miss Lightstone.

"The extra!" Margie exclaimed. "Maybe it's the extra!"

Whispers swept through the room: *The extra! The extra? The extra!* We braced ourselves for the entry of the extra, all of us craning our necks toward the door, some of us half out of our seats in anticipation.

"Sit down, Renaldo," Ruby warned. "I can't see!"

"What's taking so long?"

I was wishing it could be Antonio. I was wishing I could go back to that day when he was the new student.

Already, in my mind, I was thinking, *One time a new student arrived . . .*

THE EXTRA

~

When the door reopened, Miss Lightstone entered, followed by a girl wearing a white sweater and puffy blue skirt. She looked like an angel with her dark curly hair all around her face and daylight streaming in from the window behind her.

"This," Miss Lightstone said, "is Kalifa. You might have questions, but let's not bombard her, okay? She is not as fluent in English as you are."

I wanted to be in Kalifa's mind, to know what she was thinking and feeling.

"Do you want to say anything?" Miss Lightstone asked Kalifa.

Kalifa looked slowly around the room. Her gaze was direct, taking in each of us. At last she said, "I will try to understand you."

"I could help!" Renaldo volunteered.

"Me, too!" Freddy and four or five other boys added.

At lunch someone asked her if she was afraid, being in a new country and a new school.

"Afraid? No, not. This much better here."

Several times that day, she repeated, "This much better here." Once she added, "No hiding from soldiers with guns and knives."

All day long, I watched Kalifa and wondered where she had come from and what her life had been like, and all day long I wondered what

Antonio had thought and felt on his first day in our class, and I wondered why no one had ever called him son.

THE SUBSTITUTE

~

That Wednesday, Miss Lightstone was absent.

I knew something was wrong even before I entered the classroom because students who had arrived earlier had come back out into the hall looking worried.

"I don't want to go in."

"I feel sick."

"You're not going to believe—"

"It's a substitute."

"So?"

"Go see."

I looked in. It was bad.

It was the dreaded pointy teacher from last year.

Renaldo, who had had an even worse time with her than I did, fled to the nurse's office. "I can't do it," he said. "I just can't."

The pointy teacher—I'll call her Miss P. because I can't bear to write her name—was staring at instructions that Miss Lightstone had left. "I don't get this at all," she said.

Freddy went to the board and wrote:

> It's Wednesday. Silent Day.

Miss P. scowled.

Freddy added:

> On Wednesdays we don't talk.
> We write.

"Nonsense," Miss P. said, shuffling through more papers on the desk.

Freddy underlined *We write* and turned to us

228

and mouthed the word "Now!"

Most of us quickly got out our notebooks and began writing. Only a few, like Ruby, seemed unsure and hesitated.

Miss P. was agitated. Her skinny fingers flipped papers and her skinny arms flapped and her pointy nose wrinkled and her pointy teeth shone.

We wrote.

Her pointy shoes click-clacked as she marched around the room, peering over shoulders.

"What's that you're doing?" she asked Arif.

Bravely, he pointed to the board and put a finger to his lips.

"I asked you a question! Answer me."

Arif whispered, "It's Wednesday, it's Silent Day, and we write. We don't talk."

"Ridiculous!" she said.

We kept writing, all of us except for Ruby, who sat there with her notebook open but her hand poised midair, frozen.

Miss P. continued marching around the room, peering at our papers, until she stopped at Freddy's desk. She snatched up his notebook and held it close to her pointy face.

"What in the world? 'Stuckity stuck stuck'? This is *nonsense*! Close your notebooks. Now. This instant!"

And so we did, and then we listened to her lecture on sentence structure for the remainder of the period, and I wanted to crawl into a hobbit hole and hide.

The next day, I begged to stay home from school, but my parents said that was "not an option."

"Think of it this way," Mom said, "when Miss Lightstone does return, you'll have something interesting to write about. You can turn Miss P. into an evil character."

Half the class was absent that day.

But Miss Lightstone had returned, and those of us who were present practically drooled our relief and gratitude.

The following day, the school principal sat in on our class.

"Just happy to observe," she said. This was the same principal who had been so understanding about my encounter with the angels a few years earlier. I liked her.

But at lunch, the rumor went around (started by Ruby?) that the principal had received complaints about Miss Lightstone's teaching, and that was why she was observing our class.

THE ANNOUNCEMENT

At the end of the next day, Miss Lightstone said she had an announcement to make. She looked so serious. I feared that she was going to say that she was leaving, and I didn't think I could bear it.

"I am sorry to say—"

"Please don't say you're leaving," Margie blurted. "Please don't say that."

Others, who might not yet have feared that was going to be her announcement, gasped.

"What? What?"

"You're leaving?"

Miss Lightstone said, "Well, I am glad to see that some of you might mind if I left."

"All of us," Renaldo said. "I bet all of us would mind."

"But that is not my announcement," Miss Lightstone said. "I am not leaving."

Great relief all around. Several people clapped.

"I am sorry, though, to tell you that Antonio will not be returning."

"No—"

"Aw, no—"

"Don't say that."

Gerald asked who Antonio was.

Miss Lightstone looked as sad as I felt. "Antonio used to sit where you are sitting now."

I felt as if air was leaking out of my body, deflating me like a punctured balloon.

In answer to the chorus of *Why?* Miss Lightstone

said that she did not know why Antonio was leaving, and in answer to a chorus of *When?* she said,
"Apparently he has already moved."

"What?" Arif said. "Already?"

I may have bleated like a pitiful lamb:
"Already?"

Others chimed in:

"Without saying goodbye?"

"Really already?"

"Didn't he like it here?"

"Didn't he like *us*?"

Kalifa looked alarmed. "Did soldiers come?"

"No, no," Miss Lightstone reassured her. "No
soldiers, don't worry."

At home that afternoon, when I told Dad about
Antonio's departure, he said, "That would explain
the moving truck, then. It came this morning. I
went over to see if I could help but no one was
around, other than the movers. No grandmother,

no Antonio, no Princess What's-her-name."

I couldn't believe it. "But not to say anything? Just to leave—"

"Well, there was this in our mailbox, with your name on it," he said, handing me a small package wrapped in newspaper and tied with twine. "No postage on it, so someone must have put it there for you."

Inside was a small, carved blue frog. As I held it loosely in my palm, my thumb automatically stroked the smooth back.

A short note was attached:

This is for Gina. Antonio made it and wants her to have it. You hold it in your hand and it calms you.

    Carlotta (Princess Azalea)

It felt comfortable in my hand, something smooth and solid to hold on to.

That night, I remembered a recent update from Nonna Filomena about Angel Lucia:

Angel Lucia has been so busy in our little village. It is always so in November when people become crotchety and rude because of the cold and the dark.

One day she let loose a dozen puppies in the town square and another day she left an accordion on the steps of old Signor Franconi and a basket of warm bread on the steps of Mama Giordo and a violin on the steps of Signora Pesto.

So: Angel Lucia does not always throw pine cones or hail or knock people on the head. Sometimes she brings puppies and bread and music.

And it works. People feel better.

WHAT I SAW

~

Late that same day, as darkness fell, I saw a
strange sight from our front window. A large,
gray, lumpy figure was moving slowly along, and
on its shoulders was a small blob of blue.

The elephant and the frog?

When I opened the door, the large figure
and the small blob both waved. It was Mr. Clafferty, bundled in a gray raincoat, and perched
on his shoulders was one of the littles in a blue
jacket.

Trailing behind them was their tiny yippy-yappy dog, with its fur sticking up at odd angles. In its mouth was its own floppy, red leash.

Was this the porcupine eating red licorice?

And then I thought of the pair of sheep, gray and dirty, that Antonio had seen, and the clump of sheep Gerald had drawn, his vision of so many of us perhaps, all smiling or all not smiling, all blathering away.

I was not sure what the pancake light and the red flowers dripping pollen—that first vision Antonio shared with me—resembled, but maybe I would discover that in time.

I wanted to peer into Antonio's future and see what he would become.

THE EXCHANGE

~ૐ~

One day in class I wrote again about *mångata*, the moon's light trail upon the water, and it occurred to me that both the moon and the water needed each other to create this stunning effect. Without the water, the moon was merely a bright light in the sky. Without the moon, the water was but a dark, blank void.

When Miss Lightstone asked for voluntary contributions, I offered to read mine. There was an eerie silence when I finished, and I felt uneasy. Was it dumb what I had written?

Renaldo said, "I guess it's obvious now that you said so, but I never really thought of it that way."

Freddy said, "It's the combination of the two, right? The combination is what makes it special."

Miss Lightstone rested one finger on her chin. "Hm. Yes. The moon amplifies the beauty of the water, and the water amplifies the beauty of the moon." Her slowly emerging, full-on smile was so like Antonio's.

It worked. I felt better.

Does it seem sappy to mention it?

A person is more than a smile.

I know that.

When I revised that piece about *mångata*, I ended like this:

And I know that the moon is magnificent on its own and doesn't *need* the water, and the water is appealing all by itself and doesn't *need* the moon. But together, ah! So rich.

ONWARD TIME: TWENTY YEARS LATER

~

A month after Antonio left, I received a post-card from him, saying he wished he had had time to say goodbye to everyone, but he hadn't known he would be leaving for good. A few months later, he sent a letter explaining that his grandmother had been ill and they had had to move in with an uncle in upstate New York. This time he included an address so that I was able to reply.

We have exchanged letters for twenty

years—sometimes every few months, sometimes less often. I did not see him again until college, but soon we will be living in the same town. Antonio is a playwright, best known so far for the play *Mångata* and for the distinct imagery in his works: elephants with frogs, porcupines with licorice, rapidly growing plants, swooping lights, moons and lakes.

Margie, Arif, Freddy, Renaldo and I have remained friends, although we are spread out across the country, meeting up from time to time. It is easy enough to tell you what has become of them, but it would require at least a whole book about each to record all the ups and downs and twisty roads that got them to this place now, this time now, and to the complex individuals they have become. But the brief version is this:

Margie is a kind and thoughtful friend and a lunar researcher for NASA, and Arif is an activist and journalist specializing in environmental issues. His mission is nothing less than to save the planet.

Freddy studied drama and worked as a waiter while appearing in several off-Broadway plays, one of which starred Antonio's cousin, Carlotta. Last year, he got his big break and appeared in his first film, a comedy. I think we'll be seeing a lot more of him onscreen.

Renaldo became an English teacher and married Kalifa (the extra) and both work in the same school we attended when Miss Lightstone was our teacher.

Miss Lightstone is now Mrs. Fortuna and has three children. She is still a teacher in our old school, inspiring students every day. My life, and I suspect the lives of many others, pivoted on that year with her.

From time to time, I hear about Audrey, who is a rock singer in a band called Running

Redheads, and Ruby, who manages a rescue facility for aging horses.

Gerald is a cartoonist. I see his cartoons (*Sheeplandia*) each day in the newspaper.

No one seems to have heard from Claire since we were in school together.

Mr. Blue, the cat, died of old age, as did the Clackertys' yippy-yappy dog.

Some of the Clackerty-Claffertys still live on our old street. I've heard that one of them is now a chef, another is a grocer, and others include a fireman, a pilot, a waitress, and a librarian. One is in prison. They all have lots of children.

Uncle and Auntie Pasta are definitely not invisible. They are creating havoc in a nursing home. Uncle still wants his pasta and Auntie still wants to make it, because that is how she communicates, she says: "If you love people, you make them pasta." She is no longer allowed in the nursing home kitchen without supervision, though, because of the fires she started. Accidentally.

My parents are taking a year off from their jobs and are staying in Italy with Nonna Filomena, who is ninety-nine years old and continues to update me on Angel Lucia's actions. Most recently, Angel Lucia tossed mice down the chimney of the Luigi brothers because they poisoned the cat of Signora Fibocino.

Miss Judy retired. She and Miss Marlene are active in women's rights groups, are studying Japanese, taking yoga classes, and fostering two or three (it varies) dogs from the local animal shelter.

As for me, Gina Filomena: I am a writer, a novelist. One of my books is about a family like the Clackertys, one features an Italian nonna, one is about an eccentric angel, and several include great teachers. The moon and water (rivers, lakes, streams, oceans) seem to surface in nearly everything I write.

You've just read one of my books. All those stray pieces and *one time*s float around in me. I am learning that most of us have an intense need to communicate, but that we do it in different ways. I am also learning that people come and go, but that many will leave a piece in you and shape or influence you for years to come. You, too, will leave a piece in them.

When Antonio read a draft of this book, he said, "It's like the moon is shining down on the ocean of you."

Maybe my next book will be about a boy who was never called son.

For a long time, I thought I did not want to be married. I like my independence. But lately, I've been rethinking that.

Antonio and I, we are like the moon and the water, and maybe we would make a good pair.

You think?

Meanwhile, I wonder about you:

Who are you?
Who could you be?

～

I want to be improbable beautiful and afraid of nothing,
as though I had wings.

—MARY OLIVER

SOURCES OF FIRST LINES THAT
MISS LIGHTSTONE INTRODUCED IN HER CLASS:

1. "There is no lake at Camp Green Lake," from *Holes*, by Louis Sachar. New York: Frances Foster Books, Farrar, Straus and Giroux, 1998.

2. "Rendi was not sure how long the moon had been missing," from *Starry River of the Sky*, by Grace Lin. New York: Little, Brown & Co., 2012.

3. "In a hole in the ground there lived a hobbit," from *The Hobbit*, by J. R. R. Tolkien. New York: Houghton Mifflin, 1966.

4. "We didn't always live on Mango Street," from *The House on Mango Street*, by Sandra Cisneros. New York: Vintage Books/Random House, 1984.

5. "We think they took my papi," from *Harbor Me*, by Jacqueline Woodson. New York: Nancy Paulsen Books/Penguin Random House, 2018.

6. "My name is Elizabeth but no one's ever called me that," from *How I Live Now*, by Meg Rosoff. New York: Wendy Lamb Books/Random House, 2004.

7. "I have not had so good of a week," from *Clementine*, by Sara Pennypacker. New York: Hyperion, 2006.

HEARTWARMING BOOKS BY
SHARON CREECH!